HEDSHOT

a mystery

David W. Barber

*In a small town with secrets, a jaded journalist uncovers
a scandal some powerful forces would kill to keep hidden.*

□INDENT
PUBLISHING
IndentPublishing.com

HEDSHOT

Print edition first published in Canada in 2023
ebook edition published 2023

Cover design by McNeill Design Arts

Indent Publishing
indentpublishing.com
contact@indentpublishing.com

Canadian Cataloguing in Publication Data

Barber, David W. (David William)
HEDSHOT

ISBN 978-1-998904-04-4

Cataloguing data available from Library and Archives Canada

Author's Note

Although it's loosely inspired by some actual events in the past, I had not meant this to be a historical novel. I'd intended it to be at least roughly contemporary. I finished writing it in our current world of the covid pandemic – of variants, vaccines, lockdowns, mask wearing, hand washing, physical distancing and more. And sadly of so many people still getting sick and dying. But I'd started thinking about this story and writing it several years before all that. In the end, it seemed easier just to ignore covid, rather than try to rewrite the whole novel to include it.

So I guess that's where we're at now: We're all writing either historical novels (non-covid) or dystopian ones (with covid). There's not much in between, at least outside of fantasy or science fiction.

And it should go without saying that this *is* a novel, a work of fiction only loosely (very loosely) based on any real persons, places or events. With that in mind, it seems appropriate to borrow, with the greatest respect, remarks Robertson Davies makes about his 1951 novel, *Tempest-Tost*, the first in his Salterton trilogy:

"All characters in this story are imaginary, and no reference is intended to any living person. Readers who think that they can identify the creations of the author's fancy among their own acquaintance are paying the author an extravagant compliment, which he acknowledges with gratitude."

It remains for me to thank Jacques Lauzon and Indent Publishing for believing in this as in all my previous books. And to thank early readers including my brother Bruce and friends Julie, Mary Anne, Brett and Wilson for their observations and helpful advice.

– DWB, Toronto, 2023

Chapter 1

The waves of death compassed me
and the floods of ungodliness made me afraid.
— Psalm 18, v. 4

The problem, obviously, was what to do with the body.

Killing her had been easy enough, but what then? What to do with a hundred-and-some pounds of flesh and bone and blood?

Especially the blood. He had no idea there'd be so much blood. It was –

– My cellphone rang. I put down the mystery I was reading to look at the call display.

The custodian from the church. My temporary gig.

Why would he call late on a Friday night? Not your chatty type.

The cell rang again, I tapped to answer it.

"Heywood." (Old habits die hard: Even now I sometimes answer with just my surname, like in the newsroom.)

"Mr. Heywood," said the reedy voice on the other end, "It's Tom Pulaski."

Tom – Tomas, but he goes by Tom – is one of those no-nonsense, salt-of-the-earth types you wish the world had more of. A movie cliché if he hadn't been the real thing. Nothing flashy, just quiet and good at his job, as handyman and building superintendent. The fancy church term is sexton. He keeps the clunky old boiler heating in winter and the fans turning in summer and prevents a beautiful but drafty old stone building from collapsing in on itself.

"What's up, Tom? Is there a problem?"

"Sorry to bother you at home," he said, "but I think you should get over here."

A tremor in his voice made me uneasy.

"The police and paramedics are here already, but I think you might want to be here too," he said. "I've found a body near the choir room.

"I'm really sorry, Mr. Heywood. It's Ms. Patel. She's dead."

Chapter 2

My heart overfloweth with a good matter:
I recite my verses for the king.
My tongue is the pen of a ready writer.

— Ps. 45, v. 1

I hadn't intended to become a church musician. It just happened that way.

I'm not what you'd call religious. Not in the formal sense. I come from a long line of Unitarians – who tend to be, let's just say, pretty lax in their beliefs. Open and tolerant, but hard to pin down on any specifics. Like trying to thumbtack a blob of mercury, someone once said. But even that was too much structure for me. So I'm an agnostic lapsed Unitarian – more lapsed than which it is hardly possible to be. Agnostic because I don't even have enough faith to be an atheist. Still hedging my bets.

By training and temperament I'm a writer and editor. I've spent most of my adult life so far as a newspaper journalist. Not sure whether journalism has made me skeptical or skepticism led me to journalism. Probably both.

As George Carlin used to say, inside every cynic is a disappointed idealist.

Hadn't intended to become a journalist, either, come to that. Studied music at university because I enjoyed it and found it interesting. Mostly even fun. Was lucky to do so back when picking a career didn't seem so crucial. Or maybe just too young and stupid to have thought that far ahead.

But I soon realized that being a professional musician – especially in early music, a singer at the mercy of the slightest sniffle – would not likely be lucrative. So I ditched the idea of a music career.

Just kind of fell into journalism, first freelance and then for nearly two decades as a reporter and copy editor at *The Grayston Gazette*, the local smalltown rag. Not a whole lot smarter to have joined the dead tree industry when print journalism was already showing signs of dying a slow death. Jumping from the frying pan into the fire? More like teach a man to fish, then hand him a bicycle. Another one of God's little jokes, assuming there is one. God, that is. Plenty of jokes to go around. What's that Frost poem?

Forgive, O Lord, my little jokes on Thee
And I'll forgive Thy great big one on me.

The *Gazette* has – or had – a long and proud history as a fine, small, independent daily newspaper punching above its weight. But then its publisher, the last bastion of the family who had owned it for three generations, sold the paper – some would say sold out – to Blackwell Holdings Inc., a big chain.

Cue the jokes about falling down a deep, black well.

I'd stayed on after the takeover, not happy about it. I should have up and quit, just on principle. Who wants to work for a big, faceless, greedy corporation like Blackwell? But mortgage payments and the lousy job market had forced me to hang tight. As one does.

But I started looking around. I'd already been exploring the idea of taking over my friend Bill Garner's church gig so he could take a year off for travel and research. It's a side gig for him too, from teaching English at the university. Call it a sabbatical from the newsroom. A little leave of absence. A change of scenery to recharge my batteries, revive my flagging enthusiasm for my failing but still-beloved profession.

Then almost a year ago, in one of those cosmic coincidences that makes me think maybe there is a God after all, I lost my newspaper job – corporate "restructuring," they called it, ha! – and agreed to take over as St. Quentin's music director all in the same week. Enticed more by the music and the chance for a change than by any theology, for sure.

The gig doesn't pay much. But then neither do newspapers. After some legal wrangling, my lawyer made Blackwell pay me a severance or be sued for wrongful termination. Part of the severance package was, in a wonderful bit of corporate bafflegab, what they euphemistically called "outplacement" counselling. Grayston certainly had no other newspaper jobs on offer, and the idea of leaving town didn't appeal. Maybe the counsellors would have some suggestions on a career transition.

But no. After a bunch of interviews, Q&A questionnaires filled with more bafflegab and whatnot came the verdict:

"Mr. Heywood, you're ideally suited for a career in journalism."

Well, gee. Thanks. This just in: Water is wet.

So Bill Garner's offer of the church gig had come at the perfect time. Not to mention the legal settlement. With whatever I could pick up on the side freelancing, I had enough to keep me going for a while. If I was careful.

And now that I was beginning to settle in to the new job, I realized maybe Blackwell had actually done me a favor.

A change is as good as a rest, they say. Overall, the church gig has been much less demanding than my old newspaper one. Certainly the hours are fewer and more civilized. It's been a new challenge to revive my long-dormant musical chops. My keyboard skills – at the piano and organ, not the computer – never great at the best of times, were certainly getting a workout, both in rehearsals and services. I was even getting back into a little composing, something I hoped to explore more fully now that I had a bit more time and a choir to workshop and perform with.

So maybe my enforced departure from journalism – at least in a formal sense – had ended up being a good thing after all. I don't think I'll ever lose my instinct for curiosity, for wanting answers to life's questions big and small, for appreciating and even celebrating good people and the work they do while also wanting to hold the rich and powerful to account for their outsized sway and misdeeds. Nor did I want to lose my affection and respect for the profession at its best and my lament for its obvious decline in recent years and decades.

Despite its faults – and there are many – I still feel journalism is valuable and necessary. In today's polarized political and ideological climate – with its penchant for outright lies, for cheap tricks and clickbait – maybe more so than ever. So even if I didn't have a newsroom to work in, in some sense I still considered myself a journalist at heart.

Theologically, spiritually, philosophically, romantically, though, I was still adrift. Losing loved ones will do that to you. Especially losing them in what can only seem like such a senseless manner. Talk about a test of faith. So I sometimes feel a little guilty being a church musician but not in any meaningful way a believer. Does that make me a hypocrite, sitting at the organ or leading the choir in hymns and psalms and anthems – most of them with texts from or inspired by the Bible – wanting to convey their message as clearly as possible while yet believing none of it? Probably it does.

But even for me of little faith there's still so much beauty to appreciate, even rejoice in. The glorious and heartfelt music, obviously. (Heartfelt for others, at least. For me even just as an artistic exercise.) But also the wisdom and poetic language of the psalms and other readings. On a good day, maybe even I could find something to think about in the texts or the sermon. Not to mention the beautiful architecture – the old stones, the handsome carved wood, the stained glass. Yes, even some of the traditional pomp and theatrics.

Maybe for me, for now, that would have to be enough.

St. Quentin's Episcopalian Church – named for Quentin, or Quintinus, the third-century French patron saint of locksmiths and tailors and, appropriately for its choir, also the saint invoked against coughs and sneezes – has a small and in these increasingly secular times shrinking congregation. Not even 125 on the official list, and on most Sundays barely half of those might show up. But the congregation is active, with church groups holding meetings in the church hall, or the sanctuary itself, through the week. All sorts of others, from youth groups to the local save-the-whales crowd, hold meetings there too, which helps bring in money from renting the space. So the building is in use nearly every night of the week. I didn't think there was anyone using it this night – there often isn't on a Friday – but wasn't sure.

Part of Tom's job is to check regularly in case of burglars, vandals or other damage. But if there were a broken window or basement flooding, Tom wouldn't call me. He'd just deal with it himself. He might call the minister or maybe one of the church wardens, whose duties include looking after upkeep. Looking after in the sense of overseeing or supervising. Couldn't really see either of them getting in there with a hammer or mop and pail to do any actual work.

Well, one maybe. He's a pretty good guy who'd probably roll up his sleeves to help out. But the second, newer warden, who'd switched churches from the bigger one in town, is a fancy lawyer just elected to city council. Thinks way too much of himself, though he can pour on the charm when it suits him. Speaking of suits, his are expensive. Or sometimes he'll sport a nautical-looking navy blazer and white ducks to play commodore with his rich pals down at the yacht club.

I couldn't imagine him getting his hands dirty. Metaphorically, maybe. Not literally.

So unless some of the neighborhood bad boys had torched the choir library, or marauding mice had chewed through the wiring of the old organ, any problems Tom might discover wouldn't be ones he'd bring to me. I was, after all, only the music director. And a temp at that.

But this was different. This was a member of my choir.

And it was Priya.

Chapter 3

He bringeth forth the clouds
from the ends of the world
and sendeth forth lightnings for the rain.

– Ps. 135, v. 7

It's only a few blocks to the church from the charming old red brick house that houses my condo, so normally I walk.

I was tempted now to drive, just to save time. But there'd be cop cars, paramedics, who knows what else. Easier to walk. I thought of taking my shepherd/husky, Wolf, but decided no. She'd only get in the way, or I'd have to tie her up outside. I made sure she had food and water before heading out.

I was glad for the walk to give me some time to clear my head and think. Still reeling from the news.

Priya Patel is – was – bright and pretty and funny and clever and talented and *nice*. A winning smile and more brains than most two people put together. Also a really good musician. I was lucky to have her in my choir.

Maybe she'd just fainted. Maybe when I got there, she'd be laughing with Tom and apologizing for giving him a scare.

Yeah, right.

It was cold, windy and dark. The early November wind coming off the lake was carrying some rain, with the threat of more.

I walked up the street that borders the big park to the north and west of my place. In the daytime, in good weather, the park is popular, busy. People walking their dogs, throwing footballs, kicking soccer balls, eating lunch on the benches and picnic tables. But this time of night, this time of year, it was grim, dark, almost deserted. A few hardy people walking their dogs. (Any park, pretty much anytime – people walking their dogs.)

In the other direction, off a few blocks to my right, its bright copper spire long since weathered verdigris green, the big Episcopalian church, St. Nicholas. A light shone on a cross at the peak of the spire. Even though not fully a cathedral – a bigger city in the diocese has the cathedral seat – St. Nick's is many times larger and fancier than my own small church, both building and congregation. With the prestige, influence and money that go with it. Even now, in our relatively godless society, you can find many of Grayston's rich and powerful Episcopalian families there on a Sunday morning. If only to make sure they're being seen by all the right people.

Closer to the waterfront, in similar copper green, a dome. The city hall, its own lights shining on an old-fashioned wrought-iron weathervane. The standing joke: At St. Nick's they worship the cross. At city hall they must worship the weather. Or roosters.

Grayston, a small city of 40,000 or so with a smalltown feel on the shores of a big lake, lives up to its name. Or down, depending.

The British soldiers who stole it from the French who'd stolen it from the native peoples thought they were naming it for the regimental commander who'd won them the battle. Lord High Fooferaw III, Baron Grayston. Or whatever his name was.

But that was just a coincidence. One of the universe's little jokes. *Ba-dm-bmp.*

It's just a grey, stony place, built on bedrock and using stone for most of its oldest, most important buildings. The city hall, the old jail, the churches, the small university campus, many of the big old homes for the city's wealthy and powerful – all built of the abundant local grey stone.

The resulting piles are impressive, even imposing and often beautiful. When the leaves turn in the fall the old downtown can be gorgeous. But come winter there's a kind of institutional, dreary sameness to all that stone. Stone buildings, grey pavement, the cloudy sky reflecting grey in the rough pewter waters of the lake – a rainy winter afternoon could probably make Rebecca of Sunnybrook Farm feel morose.

I had to stop this. Too morbid. Thinking that way wasn't going to help. Wouldn't bring Priya back.

Priya is – was, had been – more than just a friend and chorister. She'd been my girlfriend for almost a year. But that was several years ago. We'd had a good relationship. It just hadn't worked out.

We'd parted well and remained friends. I was glad she'd stayed in the choir to help keep the section on track. For nearly three years now, while my own love life had stalled, she'd had a new boyfriend – a big, athletic guy named Dev.

When I got to the door of the church hall, beside the main building, I had to stop for a moment. As a newspaper reporter I'd seen my share of gruesome sights – car accidents, fire victims, even knife and gunshot wounds a few times. Never pleasant, but I'd always managed to stay in control. But those were all strangers and I'd had the job to focus on.

This was different. This was someone I had known, had cared for. I wasn't there as a reporter. I was there as a friend. I took a breath and walked in.

Chapter 4

*With the pure thou shalt show thyself pure
and with the perverse thou shalt deal accordingly.*
– Ps. 18, v. 28

The place, as the pulp writers would say, was crawling with cops.

Well, four anyway – two uniforms and a detective, and a woman taking pictures. I took her to be a police photographer, since I didn't recognize her as a photog from the paper. Probably one or two paramedics around somewhere too.

Maybe not "crawling," but more law enforcement than Macmillan Hall usually sees on any given day.

Built in the 1930s beside the main church building – that dates from the 1880s – Macmillan Hall is, like St. Quentin's itself, a handsome stone building of high ceilings, beautiful old carved oak trim and stained-glass and leaded windows, dark now with the night outside.

Past the cloakroom/entryway, the main room holds meetings during the week, choir practices Thursday nights and that venerable church tradition, the coffee/tea hour after the service each Sunday morning. On the middle of the far wall opposite the main door was a door leading to the small kitchen, where the church auxiliary makes the tea and coffee and sometimes prepares meals for that other venerable church tradition, the potluck supper, usually to raise money for some cause or other.

In the left corner of the room on the far side, another door led to a small vestibule, with a connecting door to the courtyard that leads to the sanctuary and a staircase to the second floor. Up there is a smaller choir room with an old upright piano, also the music director's cramped office. My temp digs.

The cop photog was taking pictures in the vestibule, so that was probably where the body was. I walked over to get a better look through the doorway.

As I got there the two paramedics were just finishing putting the body, already in its zip-up body bag, on the collapsible stretcher. Calm, deliberate, efficient but not rushed. I knew it was too late to hope Priya might still be alive. They'd put what looked like Priya's coat and purse, presumably found beside her body, in a clear plastic bag placed underneath the stretcher. Evidence? Or just personal effects to return to the family?

"May I help you, sir?" It was one of the two uniformed cops, one I didn't recognize, taking me gently but firmly by the elbow and leading me back into the main hall.

"It's OK, Liu," said another voice, behind me, before I could even reply. This voice I did recognize, even before I saw him coming toward us. The other uniformed officer, Don Patterson.

"Officer Liu Kang, this is Dugan Heywood," Patterson said. "He's the music director here at the church. The victim, Ms. Patel, was a member of his choir."

Kang relaxed his hand off my elbow and offered it to shake, still reserved but more friendly now that his partner had cleared me.

"I'll take responsibility for Mr. Heywood, Liu," Patterson said. "There are some questions I want to ask him anyway."

Officer Patterson – broad-shouldered, his sandy brush cut just turning grey and at nearly six feet a few inches taller than I am – took me over to the far end of the room, where Tom the sexton was sitting talking to the other police official in the room, Detective Andy Silipo. Shorter than Patterson, balding and overweight

I didn't know Silipo well, but I recognized him from his many years on the force and from stories the paper had done on his cases over those years.

Silipo was sitting on the piano bench with the piano behind him. Tom was sitting across from him on one of those stackable metal chairs with the curved laminated wooden seats you find in schools and church halls everywhere. Tall, wiry, a little stooped but still strong, bright-eyed and sharp, Tom was past 70 and had been sexton at the church for nearly two dozen years, after retiring from the army and taking an early pension.

If Silipo saw us approaching, he didn't acknowledge it. He just kept on as if we weren't there.

"OK, Mr. Pulaski," Silipo was saying, "let's just go over it one more time to make sure we've got everything. What time was it when you found the body?"

"It was just after 10, I guess," Tom said

"I know 'cause the wife and I had been watching a movie on TV and it had just ended and the early news came on. I'd already seen the news at 6, so I decided to come over and check the building."

Tom's voice was quiet, a bit tired. He'd probably been through this all at least a couple of times before.

But he went through it again. It was like this:

Priya had phoned Tom, asked if she could come over to

use the upstairs choir room to do a little practising before Sunday's service.

The church has had burglaries over the years, so officials had realized there were too many copies of the keys floating around. After the last break-in, Tom changed all the locks and church officials began to tightly control access to any keys.

Only a handful of people – the minister, the sexton, two church wardens and the music director – have keys to the building. Choir members, members of the ladies' auxiliary or anyone else wanting access had to get a key from one of us. Choir members joke that security is so tight they should change the name from St. Quentin to San Quentin. We even have wardens.

If you wanted into the building after hours, usually it was easiest just to go through Tom, who lived with his wife, Vera, in an apartment in the old manse across the street.

"Ms. Patel phoned me at about 6:30 – we were just finishing dinner – and she came by about 7," Tom said.

"She said she'd be at least a couple of hours, so I asked her to check in with me before she left, so I could lock up after her."

The hall's main door locks with a deadbolt you can turn from the inside, but once you leave the building you need a key to lock it again from the outside, so Tom would need to do that. The old spring lock was easier, but not as sturdy and too many people had accidentally locked themselves out. The deadbolt was stronger and safer.

"I distinctly remember locking the door after I let her in," Tom said. "I'm careful about that sort of thing."

I'm sure he had. There was no danger of Priya being

locked in. If she had to get out in a hurry, the deadbolt on the main door can open from the inside, and on the other side of the building there's an emergency fire exit with a crash bar and an alarm that will let you onto the side lawn. It opens only from the inside. The door to the courtyard has a deadbolt too. But going out that door would leave you stranded in the courtyard. Unless you had the key to get into the church.

By about 10, Tom was worried he hadn't heard from Priya, so he decided to check.

"So I came over here," Tom said, "and let myself in – the door was still locked and the alarm from the emergency exit wasn't going off, so I figured she must still be here. But I didn't hear her singing or nothing – and when I came into the vestibule and turned on the light, there she was, sprawled at the bottom of the stairs."

"And what did you do then?" Silipo asked.

"Well, I wasn't sure if she was dead or just knocked out, so I went over to see if I could help her. But I could tell right away there probably wasn't anything I could do.

"I wasn't a medic in the army, but I do know a little bit about first aid. I checked for a pulse and there was none. There was a big bump on her head, she wasn't breathing and it looked to me like her neck was broken. I called 911 for the paramedics anyway, though, because maybe there was something they could do. And I guess 911 called the police. And here we are."

Tom closed his eyes and gave a small sigh. I couldn't tell if he was just tired or if he was about to well up. Maybe a little of both.

"The call came in at 10:07 p.m., sir," Patterson said to

Silipo, who turned to acknowledge us for the first time. "The 911 call to the ambulance had come about a minute before that."

"Yes, I know that, officer," Silipo replied, rubbing his eyes and speaking a little more curtly than he probably intended. He looked tired too. And probably needed a cigarette. Tom would have told him, politely but firmly, there was no smoking on the property.

"I'm Dugan Heywood," I told Silipo, extending my hand. He shook it, getting half out of his seat before plopping back down again with a small grunt.

"I'm the music director here," I said, "I'd be happy to help if here's anything you need. Priya – Ms. Patel – was in my choir, so if there are any questions I can answer, please let me know."

"Thank you, Mr. Heywood," Silipo said. "Maybe you should go with Officer Patterson here and he'll let you know if we need anything.

"I think we're finished with you here," Silipo said, turning to Tom. "Thanks for your co-operation.

"I'm going to have these notes typed up into a statement for you to come to the station and sign. But that can wait til Monday. We'll call you, OK?"

"Is it all right if I clean that vestibule?" Tom said. "We'll be having a service as usual on Sunday morning, and it ought to be looking its best."

"That'll be fine, Mr. Pulaski. We'll be done here in an hour or so and then you can get off to bed and get at your cleaning tomorrow, if that's OK."

Tom got up to leave, turning in my direction with a shy smile.

"Hello, Tom," I said. "How're you doing?"

"Oh, OK, Mr. Heywood," Tom replied. "Been better. Been worse." With that, he shuffled off to the door, probably to get back to Vera and tell her everything was as well as could be expected.

It always amazed me that, even after nearly a year since I took this church job and having known Tom for many years casually before that, he hardly ever uses my given name, despite my frequent assurances that he could, and should.

To Tom, I was still "Mr. Heywood," even though I was younger and newer to the job. And I'd told him he should call be Dugan.

But it was just Tom's nature to be a little formal, a sign of the more polite and deferential era in which he was raised.

Sometimes, when I look at the world and what it seems to be coming to – the random deaths, the violence, the murders, so much other wickedness – I think maybe it wouldn't be so bad to get back to that kind of civility, to live in a world where there was a little more respect.

Chapter 5

*I had rather be a doorkeeper in the house of my God
than to dwell in the tents of ungodliness.*

– Ps. 84, v. 11

The paramedics had already taken away Priya's body, probably delivering it to the morgue and from there to the funeral home.

Silipo had gone to talk to the police photographer. She must have also been an ID tech, because she'd been dusting the staircase handrail and surrounding area for fingerprints. The mess would annoy Tom. I wondered if that was routine, or if the police were going to mount an investigation.

"I see they're checking for fingerprints, Don," I said, turning to the cop beside me. "Does that make this a crime scene?"

"No, I don't think so, Dugan," Patterson said. I noticed he'd switched to my first name, no other police within earshot.

"We'll just take a few routine prints just to be on the safe side. But it looks to me like an accident. She just tripped and fell down the stairs. They found her coat and purse beside her on the floor. It looks like she was on her way out to leave."

I'd known Don Patterson about five years now. We'd first met under less-than-pleasant circumstance. There'd been an awful scandal at the bigger Episcopalian church in town. It was a huge story for the paper and had led eventually to charges and conviction and a prison sentence. It had left a huge rift in town and a lot of damaged people in its wake. You could still see them – they were young then but older now, some of them direct victims, some just collateral damage – drifting around town, still with signs of trauma, many not fully recovered, as if they ever could be. Like wounded birds, their song no longer as sweet as once it was.

Some were even friends of mine, or at least we'd crossed paths in the same musical circles, singing at St. Nick's or in some other choir from time to time. Or if I didn't know them well, maybe I knew someone else in the family – a brother or sister or parent. Officially a city, Grayston is really just a small town, with a lot of interconnected and overlapping social circles.

Patterson had been with the police investigation. I'd been one of several reporters and editors who'd been chipping away at the St. Nicholas story in the months before it blew up big time.

For a few weeks while we were covering it in dribs and drabs in the leadup to the big reveal, I'd even filled in as acting city editor. The fulltime city editor was backpacking around Thailand or something.

One day the phone rang, so I answered it.

"City desk."

"Is this the city editor?" said the voice at the other end.

"Yes, it is. Who's calling, please?"

So he gave me his name. It was one of the wardens at St. Nicholas church.

"When are you going to stop writing all these horrible stories about our wonderful church?" he demanded to know, his voice rising to a desperate shout. "When are you going to stop writing lies about this so-called scandal?"

Mustering all the professionalism and calm I could manage, I said coolly, "When it's over."

And he slammed the phone down in my ear.

Must have been calling from a landline. Can't do that with a cellphone these days.

Even many years later, Grayston was still feeling the effects of that big scandal. Like when you drop a stone into a stillness of a pond and the ripples spread out in circles from the centre til they fill the pond and reach the very edge.

Later, when I was filling in on the police beat, Patterson was sometimes the media liaison officer, so we'd bumped into each other often – newspaper hack meets police flack. I trusted him to give me straight answers more than I trusted some of the other cops, who were more concerned with protecting their turf and not making themselves look bad.

Like in any profession, I guess. Most journalists are decent, hard-working, honest people. But there are some I wouldn't trust to tell me the time of day if we were standing under a clock.

Since taking on this church gig, I'd gotten to know Patterson in my other professional capacity too. His son Jason was now in my choir. And both he and/or his wife, Sylvia, often came on Sunday mornings to hear their boy sing.

"You had some questions for me, Don?" I sat down on the bench of the battered old Steinway grand piano where every Thursday night I led choir practice. And where Silipo had just sat.

"Yeah, just a few routine ones," he said, taking out a little notebook and flipping to a new page. His manner became more formal. We were back to official police business. I wondered if I was "Mr. Heywood" again.

"I know you're here because Mr. Pulaski called you. What time was that?"

"Well, I'm not really sure, but it was a little before 11," I said. "I didn't really look at the time, but it was probably 10:45, around there. I could check my cellphone log if you need to know."

"Did Ms. Patel tell you she was coming here tonight?"

"Not this particular night. But she often came here on Fridays to practise, because she knew the hall would probably be free. Sometimes I'd be here myself and I'd let her in. But usually she'd just get Tom to let her in."

"And who has keys to this building?"

So I took him through it:

"The only people who have keys," I said, "are me; Tom; Hugh Parry, who's the minister; and the two church wardens, Jack Benson and Philip Sanders. They're the kind of keys you're not supposed to be able to copy easily, though I guess someone could get around that if they really wanted to. Pretty sure someone with the skills could pick the lock if they wanted to."

"Was there any special relationship that you know of between Mr. Pulaski and Ms. Patel?"

That seemed out of the blue.

"You mean like a sexual one? Some sort of affair? God, I don't think so," I said. "Tom and Vera have been happily married for nearly 50 years. And Priya didn't go for older men. At least, not that much older."

I might have blushed a little. I'm a few years older than Priya, but I don't think that's the same thing.

"How long have you known Mr. Pulaski?"

"I took the job here as music director last February," I said, "so that's been almost a year. But I've known Tom a little bit for longer than that. I'd sometimes fill in for the guy who normally has the job.

"So all together, I guess I've known Tom a little longer than I've known you. Say six or seven years."

"Would you consider him trustworthy?"

That last question threw me. I wasn't sure what he was driving at.

"Sure, he's trustworthy," I said. "What's going on, Don? I thought you said this wasn't a criminal investigation."

"Don't panic. It's OK. Like I said, it's just routine. We're just covering the bases. Everything you've told me checks out against what Mr. Pulaski said and what the paramedics reported and what we know from a cursory look at the scene where the body was found.

"We've already dusted for prints on the staircase and in that little vestibule and on the doors, just to be thorough," he said.

"The only good ones we've found belong to Ms. Patel herself and a few in the immediate vicinity of the body that probably belong to Mr. Pulaski. There are smudges on the handrail and a few other places, but they could be Ms. Patel's, too. Or anybody's, really. A church has a lot of people coming and going, I guess.

"So, listen," Patterson said. "You didn't hear this from me, but here's what the report is going to say: accidental death as the result of a fall down the stairs. That's all."

Patterson smiled and his manner softened a little.

"Listen, Dugan, I'm sorry," he said. "I know she was a

friend of yours, a good friend, and that's always hard to take. But these things happen. Don't let it get to you."

"Yeah, you're right," I said. "I guess I'd feel better if I knew *why* it happened."

"That's just it: It just *happened*. It was an accident. Look, she was already dead when the ambulance got here," Patterson said.

"She broke her neck in the fall. If it's any consolation to you, she would have died quickly and without suffering much pain. Let it go at that."

"Yeah, Don. OK." I said, with less conviction than I felt. "Are we done here? I'd like to get some fresh air."

"Sure, Dugan. Go home. There's nothing you can do here. Go walk your dog or something."

I smiled at that. Wolf is a great dog, but she'd been abused as a puppy before I rescued her. So although she's lovable and loyal with me, she doesn't much like other men until she's known them long enough. Don was one of the few men she'd taken an instant shine to. Another reason I was inclined to trust him. Wolf is an excellent judge of character.

I wasn't going to get much fresh air right outside the church hall. I could smell the cigarette as I opened the door. Silipo was half-leaning, half-sitting on the wrought-iron stair rail, puffing away, as if desperately trying to make up for lost time.

Standing a few steps below him, digital player/recorder in hand to take down every word, was Sandra Novak, an old friend from the newsroom. She must be the duty reporter tonight. She'd likely heard the police or ambulance call on the radio scanner – there's probably an app for that now –

and came over when she heard about the possibility of a body. It's a morbid business sometimes, journalism. Morbid but necessary.

Seeing me, Sandra's composure – normally cool, efficient and professional on the job – dropped a bit.

"Hey, Dugan," she said. "I've just heard about Priya. I'm so sorry. I'll talk to you later."

She turned back to Silipo, resuming her reporter's stance. I'd been dismissed. Or put on hold until she was finished doing her job.

She'd known Priya too. But she was there to represent the paper and to get a story if there was one. It didn't matter whether she knew the victim. It might make the job harder, but not impossible. In a small city like Grayston, lots of social and professional circles overlap and it seems like everybody knows everybody else. There's a standing joke about the "Grayston mafia," so keeping that professional detachment was sometimes hard. But that was the job.

Some people say journalists are too cynical and cold-hearted. I had a news editor once whose famous reaction to any story pitched at him, whether local or from the wire, was 'How many dead?' He'd half-smile, but he was only half-kidding. Most of the time, that's really what it comes down to: How many dead? How many hurt? What's the damage?

I don't think journalists are cold-hearted. Sure, like cops, they've seen more death, corruption, greed and the other seven deadly sins than most people. But that doesn't mean most journalists, like most cops, aren't still affected emotionally by the tragedies, both large and small, of everyday life. They're maybe just a little better at dealing with it. Or ignoring it and carrying on regardless. They have to be.

I excused myself, walked down the stairs and took a few more steps to get away from the entrance. I wanted to give them enough distance that it wouldn't seem I was intruding.

But not so far away that I couldn't still hear their conversation. I'd been a reporter too long to pass up the chance of getting more information. Or maybe I'm just nosy.

"So, Detective Silipo," Sandra was saying, "are the police ready to make a statement?"

"Well, Ms. Novak," Silipo said. I couldn't tell if his inflection on 'Ms.' had been condescending or not. For his sake, I hoped not. "We'll have more information for you next week after the coroner has had a chance to examine the body officially. But as the senior officer at the scene, I'm satisfied with the information we have at hand.

"The victim, Ms. Priya Asmahan Patel, age 36, died at approximately 9 p.m. this evening in Macmillan Hall of St. Quentin's Episcopalian Church. She died of a broken neck and other injuries sustained in a fall down a set of stairs. We believe her death was accidental and we have no reason to suspect foul play."

I could see Silipo smile just slightly at his own use of the term "foul play." He knew it was a cliché and he was sounding like some TV cop. But that's the thing about clichés: They become hackneyed only after people have been using them for real for quite a while. Even "hackneyed" is a cliché – a reference to something commonplace, from a workaday carriage horse.

"Ms. Patel's body was discovered shortly after 10 p.m.," Silipo said, "by Mr. Tomas Pulaski – there's no H in Tomas – who is the church caretaker, and the circumstances of her death were confirmed by paramedics of the Grayston ambulance service and by the investigating officer, Officer Don Patterson. Her next of kin have already been notified and the Grayston police department will be concluding its investigation shortly. As I said, we're considering this an accident. A tragic one, but an accident all the same.

"I don't think there's much of a story here for you, Ms. Novak," Silipo said. His tone softened slightly. No longer giving the official police line. "So why don't we all just go home and get some sleep? I promise I'll call you if the coroner turns up anything – knife wounds or cyanide or anything like that.

"That last bit was off the record, by the way!" Silipo said quickly. Nervous. Regretting letting down his guard to a reporter. Didn't want to appear callous or flippant – especially not on the record.

But Sandra just smiled. "It's OK, Detective. Don't worry, I'm not going to make you look foolish. The Patel family's going to have enough to deal with already. Just remember to tell me if you do find anything."

"I will," said Silipo. Relieved. Score one for media/police relations. Sandra had just earned some brownie points with Silipo. Never a bad thing to have up your sleeve.

Silipo went back inside, leaving Sandra and me alone. She came over and gave me a quick hug. After a moment, she pulled away slightly. "I should get back to the newsroom and write this up," she said, apology in her voice. "It's not much, but if I can call a few people for quotes I can put together a nice obit for tomorrow's paper."

Amongst themselves, journalists like Sandra and I would naturally call it an 'obit.' In polite company, we're usually more careful to use the formal, more respectful term, 'obituary.' Jargon has its place. But so does formality.

"I think Priya's parents would like that," Sandra said. "And before that I should post something online. Are you going to be OK?"

"Yeah, I'll be fine," I said. Almost meant it. "You get back to the newsroom."

"You know we're overdue for a greasy spoon breakfast. And you know where."

"You bet. And you know my new sked – busy Thursday evenings and Sunday mornings. Other than that, anytime."

"Must be nice to be 'retired,'" she said with a grin.

And then, a little awkwardly, she got out her recorder again. "Hey, before you go: Do you want to give me a quote for the obit?"

I had to smile. We'd never been in this situation before, Sandra the reporter interviewing me for a story. But she had every right to ask.

"Sure," I said, taking a moment to gather my thoughts so they'd come out right. "Priya Patel was a good friend, a fine musician and a lovely person. I'll miss her a lot, and so will many others."

"Thanks, Dugan."

I didn't envy Sandra the next few hours. Writing an obit is one of the worst tasks a reporter can have. It's not easy phoning people up and asking them on the spot to say a few nice words about their friend or family member who has just died. In the worst scenarios, the reporter is often the one who has to inform that person of the death. The police notify only the immediate next of kin, who are often too shaken to speak to a reporter anyway. I've had to do obits more than a few times myself. Never enjoyable.

So that was to be Priya's epitaph, the culmination of 36 years of living and interacting in the world: "A good friend, a fine musician and a lovely person." You could do a lot worse. I'm sure others would have more to say to round out the picture of her life.

I wonder, what would anyone say about me when I'm gone? I hope it's half as complimentary as I knew Priya would get. She deserved all the kind words.

When I got in the door after walking home, Wolf was happy to see me, wagging her tail and doing that quiet husky growl. It was after midnight, and well past time for her usual late-night walk.

I put her on leash, let her out and followed her as she trotted down the street and around the corner toward the lake, following the familiar path of her usual nighttime route. We walked along the shoreline for a while, past the site of the new condo construction, before working our way back home.

When Tom called, I'd left a fire burning in the fireplace in the smaller second bedroom I have set up as an office/study. By the time we got back from our walk, the fire had almost completely burned out. Crouching down at the glowing embers, I gave them a few pokes and stared into the red-hot glow for quite a while.

Priya. Life. Death. God – assuming there is one.

What kind of God would let such a vibrant life be suddenly snuffed out like a candle? Or turned off like the flick of a light switch? It just didn't seem fair.

Chapter 6

O my God, I cry in the daytime, but thou hearest not,
and in the night season also I take no rest.
– Ps. 22, v. 2

I didn't get much sleep that night, although I must have gotten some.

When Tom had called – not even three hours ago, but it seemed like forever – I'd been reading a mystery novel with some music in the background.

My office/study isn't as large or as bright as the living room – during the daytime the living room is light and airy and from the window you can catch just a glimpse through the other buildings of the lake – but at night I prefer to read there. The study's cozier, more compact, and the shelves surrounding me with books make me feel all erudite and philosophical, even when I'm only reading good, trashy fiction.

The books represent a lifetime of collecting and cover a wide range of topics, though most reflect either some longstanding interest – music, music history, books on language, philosophy, politics or liberal theology, books on Sherlock Holmes and a lot of other mysteries, some science fiction – or of particular areas I've had to research over the years, back when I was more active as a journalist.

It's a good room. Comfortable, especially on a lousy, cold night like this one. Makes me feel a bit like old Sherlock himself, actually. All I need is some Dr. Watson to help out and make me look clever by comparison. And maybe a housekeeper to bring the tea.

I read too many detective and mystery novels. I'll admit it. Or just ask one of my editors, who would razz me for sometimes seeing mysterious or nefarious motives where probably there weren't any. And for sometimes even letting that suspicion creep into the early drafts of my news or feature stories. Which the editor would promptly trim back. And rightly so.

But I like them. Noir and pulp novels from the '40s and '50s, more recent ones like Parker's (now Atkins's) Spenser or the Elvis Cole/Joe Pike ones from Crais. Peterson's New York tabloid guy John Wells is fun for a newshound like me. That guy Sternbergh gives them a cool sci-fi twist with Spademan. What can I say? I know I should be broadening my mind with *Emma* or *Ulysses* or *The Remains of the Day*, but I just find "literature" more than I can handle sometimes.

The heroes in detective novels – the real private eyes, anyway – usually carry a gun. Not so much the journalists. I can relate. I hate guns. A gun would scare me more than whoever I was trying to scare with it. Not a good idea. So no gun, thank you very much. Just my reporter's skills – dig around in documents and paperwork, ask people questions, sometimes until they get tired of you but hopefully until they give you the right answers, and try to put the pieces of the puzzle into some sort of coherent narrative.

Oh, and try to avoid getting sapped over the head and knocked unconscious. That seems to happen in pulp novels a lot.

When I got back home, I was emotionally exhausted but still wired, with a buzzing brain that wasn't going to let me sleep right away. Reading probably wasn't going to help, but music might. So I put another log on the fire, stoked it up to get it going again and turned the music back on.

It was Bach's *B-minor Mass*, the Rifkin one, one voice to a part (and at early pitch, almost in A minor). The pedants are still arguing, but I think it's terrific. Sure, you lose some grandeur in the big, splashy movements. But you can really follow the counterpoint in the fugues. All those craftily woven threads of melody working in and around each other – the soprano, the bass and those intricate inner voices overlapping to form a complex pattern without ever getting tangled up.

Pop music is mostly a nice tune on top with a good bass and some harmonic filler in between. Even a lot of classical music is mostly about the outer parts. But with Bach (also Byrd, Purcell, some others) it's often the inner voices that have the good stuff, make the music interesting with the crunchy dissonances and the intricate harmony. Old J.S. might have made one helluva mystery writer.

I stayed up well past 2 just listening to the Bach and staring at the fire, trying to make sense of everything that had happened. I didn't have much luck. What does that old hymn say? "God moves in a mysterious way, His wonders to perform."

I remember an old cartoon – *New Yorker* probably, maybe *Playboy,* can't remember – that shows a couple of angels on a cloud looking at an old guy with a long beard and wearing a long robe. He's on all fours facing upward, supporting himself on hands and feet, scrabbling awkwardly across the clouds. The punchline has one of the angels saying to the other: "You're right. God *does* move in a mysterious way!"

Yeah, well. I guess God moves in a mysterious way even when he *isn't* performing wonders.

There was something nagging at the back of my mind, something that didn't quite make sense, some little fact that was or wasn't there. Maybe I was wrong, maybe I was imagining it. Maybe I've read too many mystery novels or written too many stories about bad people doing crooked or sleazy things. Maybe nothing ever adds up completely and makes perfect sense.

But there was something. Something wrong, something missing, something that didn't quite fit. But damned if I could think what it was.

It's like when there's the name of a movie or an actor or a song title you should be able to remember right away but you can't. Nominal aphasia is the fancy medical term. (My speech pathologist friend tells me all sorts of interesting terminology. And if you can remember the term you probably don't have the condition.) It's right there, teasing you, but you can't think of it. Usually it just pops into your head later.

There was something like that now, but I couldn't get it. Something I'd seen or heard – or maybe hadn't seen or heard, like that Sherlock Holmes story of the dog who didn't bark in the nighttime. Something was bugging me, some little detail.

Damn.

Eventually I went to bed and managed to fall asleep. But I woke up early, as I usually do – partly because I just couldn't stop thinking about Priya's death and partly just the legacy of all those years working the early-morning shift in the newsroom.

Most people who work late nights or the midnight shift call it the "graveyard" shift. Some newspapers call it the "lobster" shift. I think it goes back to one of the old New York dailies that had its offices down by the river. Reporters and editors going to work at 3 in the morning or some awful time found themselves up with the lobster fishermen out setting their traps and nets for the day. Or maybe just because working nights makes you cold and irritable.

I got up and threw on some dog clothes – old jeans and a sweater, jacket against the wind. By a little after 6, Wolf and I were back down by the lake, going for our first walk of the day. I'm not sure who likes it more at that time of morning, the dog or me. She ran along the shoreline, barking at the gulls and sniffing the ground on the trail of squirrels or mastodons or who knows what. I stuck mostly to the pathway, sometimes veering off to keep an eye on her closer to the water, which was calmer this morning than it had been last night. The wind had died down from an overnight rain.

When it came time for her to poop, Wolf spent a long time sniffing and going back and forth and turning around before finally settling on a particular spot. What *is* it dogs are looking for when they do that? Why is one little chunk of ground – that, to a human at least, looks the same as everywhere else – any better or more attractive as an outdoor latrine than any other? And why, if it's so special, is the spot the dog picks this morning somewhere completely different from the spot she picked last night, or the one she'll probably pick later in the day?

Maybe dogs, like reporters, just like to play hunches. You

may not know exactly what you're looking for, you just sniff around until you find something interesting that feels right.

And then you crap all over it, I thought, taking the analogy to its logical conclusion and insulting my profession at the same time.

I'm sure some people really do think that's what journalists do. In most surveys, my profession ranks near the bottom, down there with used car salesmen, politicians and lawyers. I bagged the poop and took it to the nearest garbage bin. We have recycling bins, too. I keep hoping the city will give us public compost bins for food scraps and dog poop. No luck yet. Wolf was off exploring again, sniffing around for something else. On to the next story, like any good newshound. Journalism and journey, after all, come from the same root.

Sunday mornings I have my church gig but Saturdays are usually free, unless I need some extra practice now that I've traded in my computer keyboard for the musical kind. Sometimes that means just a day of puttering and cleaning and running errands. But sometimes I'm able to drive north to the country and go for a hike on my land or work on my little cabin. Especially this time of year, with the leaves changing color, it's beautiful and relaxing. After last night's tragedy, I could really use a nice, restorative walk in the country. Maybe that would clear my head.

Meantime it was time to get out on the water. That would help too. I called for Wolf, who came bounding back from whatever she'd been exploring. It was still early but soon time for more cars to be showing up on the streets, so I snapped on her leash and walked her back to home.

I quickly stripped out of my dogwalking clothes and grabbed the wetsuit, gloves and water shoes hanging in the shower, still drying from yesterday. The wetsuit's stretchy but still I had to struggle a bit to get into it. Need to lose a few pounds, I guess. I'm a good kayaker but the water was cold enough to make the wetsuit a safe choice. I put it on and went around to the back yard where I stow the kayak and its gear.

I like a canoe and I like going on a little canoe trip or two every year. One good friend and I – a real church musician, not a dilettante fill-in like me – go on a canoe trip every year that's become a great little ritual. But unless you have an expensive one, which I don't, a canoe is heavy to portage and harder to paddle on your own, especially in rough water.

The great thing about a kayak – especially a small whitewater one like mine, not a big sea kayak – is you can do it on your own. It's easy to carry and a lot easier to control when the waves get rough. If all else fails and you do go underwater, you can get yourself back up with what they used to call an Eskimo roll. I guess the better term now is kayak roll. Anyway, with any luck you wouldn't stay submerged and drown – as long as you know what you're doing.

I grabbed the spray deck that keeps water out of the boat – crucial in case of a roll – shoved the double-bladed paddle into the cockpit as far as it would go, slung the kayak and paddle over one shoulder – at less than 40 pounds it's an easy carry – and walked it down to the lake.

Chapter 7

*The same stone which the builders refused
is become the headstone of the corner.*

— Ps. 118, v. 22

My place – a small 19th-century brick mansion lately renovated into modern condo units and grandly called the Grandview – is nothing fancy but I love that it's just a short walk to the waterfront. Location, location, location, as the real estate listings always say. And just around the corner at the foot of the street is a small boat launch with a ramp and a short dock where it's easy to put in. Perfect.

A kayak on the water is maybe the most stable small boat you'll ever find. Much safer than a canoe, safer even than a little speedboat or the small or larger sailboats they use at the yacht club. You're sitting in the kayak right on the water, pretty much right *in* the water, so your centre of gravity is low. In a strong current in whitewater, or if a big wave hits you in rough water, you can tip over quite far to one side or the other without going over completely. And if you do know how to roll you can pretty much get right back up – dunked, maybe cold, but safe.

So in maybe just 10 minutes after hefting the kayak I was in the boat pushing off from shore and paddling away out into the lake.

I've always given my various cars names – my old Mini had been Winston, the jeep is Jeri in memory of my late wife. So when I bought my kayak, I named her Assignment. Even had a little brass plaque engraved and bolted it onto the deck near the cockpit. A little "in" joke: "I'm sorry, Mr. Heywood is not in the newsroom right now. He's out on Assignment."

The kayak is a near-perfectly symmetrical boat, so just to keep in practice – it's the musician in me – I paddled backwards for several boat lengths away from shore before pivoting around and heading out into open water.

The lake was still fairly calm and flat. But small ripples and waves were just starting to form as a gentle wind started to pick up. On really windy days, the lake can see big swells and choppy waves. Paddling the kayak in water that rough is risky, but I could handle it.

The sun was just rising – we were still some weeks before the winter solstice, when the days start getting longer again – but there was enough ambient light in the overcast sky that I could see the hulking mass of the new construction site behind me just to the east of the boat ramp where I'd put in. Paddling forward on one side and backward on the other, with just a few strokes I swung the boat around to look back at the shore.

The steel-and-concrete outline of what was to become the first of two big, impressive office/retail/condo towers loomed over the site, dominating the skyline. If you were on the back side of it, say in my little building, it cut you off from the waterfront like a big brick wall. For some – the developer, presumably, and certainly for the residents of the high-priced condos facing the lake who would have a spectacular view of the water – this new complex would be a thing of beauty. But for me, it stood as a monument to human stupidity, arrogance and greed.

Unlike a canoe paddle with its single blade, a kayak paddle is a shaft with a blade at each end. A trend I've noticed among newer paddlers is to have both blades facing the same direction. But my paddle was the older, traditional kind, with the two blades set at a 90-degree right angle. So when you finish a stroke on one side you're already set up to put in the blade on the other side, with just a little turn of the wrist to set up the blade perpendicular to the water.

If you forget the little wrist move, your blade will go slicing into the water rather than pushing it. Not good. Rookies will do that sometimes and lose their balance, maybe even tip over. I'm not sure whether the newer paddles make it easier or harder. Maybe it's just what you're used to. But after you've made that mistake a few times you don't usually do it again. You get the hang of it and paddling on one side and then the other in a couple of smooth motions becomes easy. Almost like walking, you don't really have to think about it.

I got into a nice, steady rhythm of paddling and soon was moving at an easy clip westward along the shore toward the hospital and the university campus beyond that. Not pushing myself, just trying to keep a nice, even pace.

Agatha Christie – grand dame of the classic English mystery novel – said she got some of her best ideas while washing the dishes. There's something about engaging part of your brain in a simple, repetitive task that frees up another part of your brain for more abstract creative pursuits. Sometimes I actually like washing dishes for that very reason. I do some of my best thinking while I'm out on the water paddling.

I started thinking about tomorrow morning's service, going over in my head what music we'd be singing. With any luck it should all be easy stuff.

And then I remembered Priya, a tiny stab at my heart, and realized we'd have to make some changes. The choir would be upset but I was sure they'd be able to pull it together to sing something in her memory. But I'd have to talk with the minister – did he even know yet? – about changing some of the service music. I'd like us to sing something fitting. Would have to figure out what that would be.

I paddled a few more strokes and tried not to think about anything at all, just concentrate on the rhythm and the physical movement of paddling on one side and then the other. The symmetry of a kayak, the balance of paddling on both sides, makes it generally easier than a canoe to keep in a straight line. There are tricks in a canoe if you're paddling solo – the J-stroke or feathering that mean you don't have to keep switching sides – but with a kayak that balance of opposing forces is built in. If only finding such balance in other aspects of life were as simple and elegant.

Dip. Pull. Wrist.

Dip. Pull. Wrist.

Gliding silently across the water, it's very soothing. After last night, just what I needed.

I tried to focus on the paddling and keep my mind clear.

But that nagging thought that had kept me awake last night came back. It wouldn't show itself, but it wouldn't go away. Something my brain was trying to tell me. But it was lurking in the shadows.

Sometimes a song or a melody will pop into your head

for no reason that seems obvious at the time. It's just there. Doesn't always mean anything. Maybe you just heard it on a passing car radio or as elevator music when you weren't really paying attention.

But the shrinks say sometimes it's your subconscious trying to send you a message. Maybe you associate the melody with someone in your life. Or the lyrics mean something in your current situation.

Maybe that's true or maybe it's just BS. But there sure was something bugging me in the back of my mind. If I ignored it and kept paddling, maybe it would come to me.

Dip. Pull. Wrist.

Dip. Pull. Wrist.

Pretty soon, thoughts and images started to flood back in. But not the answer I was looking for. Priya's smile. Her laugh. The sound of her lovely accent with its inherently musical cadence. Her gentle tears – both of us crying a little bit – when we broke up, admitting to ourselves and each other that it just wasn't going to work out. For a whole bunch of reasons, mostly small, some tangible but still difficult to define or articulate. And most of them my fault, not hers.

Priya was the first woman I'd dated after my wife and child had died. Long after. I took a long time grieving before even thinking about another relationship. But obviously not long enough. Priya was sweet and we had a good time together. But it turned out I wasn't ready to move on. Maybe I never will be.

Did I love Priya? No. Did we love each other? No. Love is big. Huge. We didn't have that. Not really. Or hadn't reached that yet. Maybe we would have gotten there, given time.

But we did have affection, even intimacy. And that counts for something. Sometimes a lot. But it hadn't been enough. Again, my fault.

So we'd parted amicably, as they say. Promised each other we'd still stay friends. Which we did. Both proud of that. Can't always be done, but we'd managed it.

Not that it matters now. She's gone. It hurt my soul, but there was nothing I could do about that.

The Saturday *Grayston Gazette* was at my door when I got back home. Quick shower, changed into regular clothes. Made tea and read Priya's obit in the bottom corner of the city front. There was no byline, but I knew Sandra had written it. I'd already read her quick online hit before going to bed, but as a print subscriber I still like to support the dying dead-tree side of the industry I grew up in. Sandra had filled it out for the print edition, with a smiling head-and-shoulders graduation portrait of Priya – a headshot (or hedshot in the lingo of the biz) – and quotes, including mine ("a longtime friend," fair enough) and from others who'd known her. Sandra had even gotten hold of Priya's mother, which would have been tough on both of them, but also probably where she'd gotten the hedshot. She'd done a nice job. I'd have to remember to tell her that.

But for now, it was Saturday morning, still early. And last night's rain had cleared, leaving the morning cool and crisp. A perfect day to get out of town and go up to the land.

Chapter 8

*Truth springeth out of the earth
and righteousness hath looked down from heaven.*

– Ps. 85, v. 11

"The land." That's what I call it. Others have "the cottage," or "the cabin" or maybe "the camp." But for me it's almost always just "the land."

Not so much in some hippie-trippy "back to the land" way. When my wife and I bought it, that's all it was – just a few acres of land, nothing but trees and a beaver pond. We couldn't afford real waterfront. Not then. Especially not now. After a few years I'd built a small cabin – officially just a storage shed. Sometimes I'll talk about "going up to the cabin." But even now it's mostly still just "the land."

"OK, Wolf, let's go! Going to the land!"

Her ears perked up. She knows that word.

I put on extra layers and hiking boots, grabbed a rain jacket just in case and got Wolf harnessed into the back of the jeep. I'd grab some breakfast on the way out of town.

Grayston is small, so pretty soon we were up past the main highway and onto the two-lane blacktop heading north. After a straight stretch, you quickly get into hills and curves as the county road winds its way around rocky outcroppings and small lakes, rising out of the lake basin as it goes.

In my 20s, I'd had on old Austin Mini 1000 – the original tiny British one, not the newer, bigger, BMW reboot – into which I'd had my mechanic put a dual-carb 1275cc Cooper engine. A stealth Cooper. Went like stink. Nothing more fun on a nice fall day like this than driving this winding two-lane road in the Cooper.

Road crews had rerouted and smoothed out some of the sharper curves over the years, making the drive a bit safer but less fun. Well, fun until it isn't. God knows I know that.

A few years ago, one of those sharp curves had taken the life of my wife and our baby daughter. I was just coming up on it now. I could rarely pass it without thinking of them. The pang gets a little less every year. But it will never go away.

I always think of it as Jeri's curve, for my wife – Jerusha, a fine Old Testament name and ironic for a woman as agnostic as I am – and our baby daughter, Chelsea.

It was one of those curves the county had since rebuilt. But even that would not have helped my wife and daughter. Better roadbuilding, crumple zones, airbags and even the best infant car seat are no match for some drunken asshole driving his giant pickup way too fast who swerves across the centre line and smashes full tilt into an oncoming car. Jeri's car.

She was always a safe driver, but even observing the speed limit she wouldn't have seen it coming. Around a curve. In the dark. In the rain.

He didn't hit her head on, more at an angle. Which made it worse. The airbags and car seat might have saved them, but the impact pushed Jeri's car off the road, down the embankment and into a swamp. Even if they'd survived the crash, they didn't survive drowning.

The drunk asshole avoided any personal responsibility –

or remorse – by smashing his pickup into a rock cut. And that was the end of him.

It was late at night. Dark. No houses nearby and no one else on the road. It was a Sunday and Jeri and I had been at the cabin for the weekend. I was still at the newspaper then, but thankfully had that weekend and a few days off. But Jeri had to work in the morning, so she'd decided to drive back into the city with Chelsea so she could get a fresh start. I was going to spend another day or so up in the woods and join them later.

No one even discovered the accident until it got light out. A passing driver saw the pickup and called police. And it wasn't until investigators got to the scene that they found Jeri's car half-submerged in the water.

By then it was way too late.

The cops ID'd the plate quickly enough. But cellphone service wasn't as good or widespread back then out in the country. They tried calling me but couldn't get through. It was a local cop – not Don Patterson or anyone I knew – who tracked me down at the cabin and broke the news. Then the trip to the morgue to ID the bodies.

Just as Priya's parents would probably have done by now.

Another 30 minutes or so up the county road comes the turnoff to the gravel road that leads to my property. Wolf had been napping in the back but woke up as I slowed down to make the turn. She knew we were getting close.

The gravel sideroad has a few curves of its own, making it tricky come winter, even when the county plow has gone through. You don't want to slide off into the ditch. But it was too early for snow – some leaves in color were still on the branches – and before long we were at my property and the little lane that leads to the cabin.

I let Wolf out of the jeep and she went running around burying her nose in the leaves and yipping happily. She likes it up here even more than I do.

I'd bought the land long before I knew Priya, back when I was still married. I should say "we" bought the land. The thing about being single, then married, then single again – by divorce or death or whatever – is the pronouns. Keeping track of the pronouns when you're telling a story – I/we, me/us mine/ours – gets complicated. Sometimes sad. (Same applies when you leave a job – voluntarily or not: Every "we" becomes a "they" But it takes your brain some time to adjust.)

Jeri and I had bought the land about 10 years ago, just after we got married, scraping together every penny we had for the down payment and mortgage.

Buying raw land with nothing on it – no cabin or cottage, not even a well or septic – is cheaper. And often buying 10 or 20 acres of unserviced recreational land is cheaper than buying a half-acre or one-acre serviced building lot. But still it's not cheap. Neither of us was making a lot of money.

But it was important, it was a dream, so we'd done it. We took a map and Jeri's compass – not the kind that points north but the kind you had as a kid in school from geometry for drawing circles – stuck the point in Grayston and drew a half-circle north, east and west (south is the big lake) in an arc we figured was about a 45-minute drive from the city. Our ideal time limit for driving there. Anything more than an hour risks becoming a chore. And who wants that?

And then we started looking, spending months reading ads and real estate listings, driving around the countryside looking at For Sale signs and even notices pinned on bulletin boards in little country stores or gas stations. Tromping around in the bush looking for fences and property lines and survey stakes, getting eaten alive by bugs and enduring more soakers than I can remember. After going it alone with no success, we hired an agent, which helped speed things up.

But even so, we looked for many more months and trudged through a lot of duds (too often "waterfront view" is real estate speak for "swampy mess," hence the soakers) before we found a property we both liked and could maybe, possibly, afford.

It was a good dream. And for a while it had seemed perfect.

And just when you think you've got it made, life throws you a loop.

How did Kierkegaard put it? Life can only be understood backwards, but it must be lived forwards.

Chapter 9

Thou also shalt light my candle.
The Lord my God shall make my darkness to be light.
— Ps. 18, v. 5

While Wolf ran around outside, I unlocked my little cabin and went inside. No burglars here. Also, thankfully, no signs of mice or chipmunks or other little creatures. Anything edible I've safely put away in glass jars or tins, but they like chewing paper too. So far, the handful of books and paper I keep up here seemed safe from damage.

It's about as basic as you can get – one room, 10x10 with a shed roof made from old barn steel that sounds great in the rain. I was able to build a lot of it with salvaged or reclaimed lumber and materials. Saving the planet, sure, but saving money too.

There's a loft bed on the high wall with a ladder, to save floor space underneath. The world's tiniest woodstove, salvaged from a friend's old ice-fishing hut, is just enough to keep it warm in the winter and take the edge off cool nights in the turnaround seasons of spring and fall. There's an outhouse with a composting toilet a little way off in the woods.

No running water, no electricity. Maybe someday I'd put up solar panels or a small wind turbine. But for now it was flashlights and battery-powered lamps and natural sunlight from the windows. Nothing fancy, but it's mine.

Outside, I whistled for Wolf and we set off down an old

path – hardly a path. Maybe an old logging road. Life is too much like a pathless wood, as Frost says.

Wolf trotted happily beside me, sometimes going off to sniff something on the side. I didn't want her wandering off too far. I've posted No Hunting signs everywhere, but the last thing I need is some bozo hunter taking a potshot, thinking she really *is* a wolf. Or shooting at a deer and having a lousy aim. If it doesn't hit anything first, a .22 rifle bullet can travel more than a mile.

You can never be too careful, so both the dog and I were wearing orange vests. Better safe than sorry.

Like Frost's, these woods were lovely, dark and deep. Not so dark with the sun starting to come through. But lovely anyway. I looked up. The branches arched overhead, close together but not quite touching – crown shyness, the arborists call it, and even they aren't sure how or why it happens – looking a bit like the ceiling of the nave, or central part of a church sanctuary.

What's that Shakespeare sonnet?

That time of year thou mayst in me behold
When yellow leaves, or none, or few, do hang
Upon those boughs which shake against the cold,
Bare ruin'd choirs, where late the sweet birds sang ...

Bare ruined choirs.

Grayston knew all about that. The tragedy at St. Nick's had nearly destroyed its music program and left tension and hard feelings that still lingered. The new music director was rebuilding, but it was a slow process.

Some of those old choir members had left and come to

my church choir. Some had just left the church entirely. Some had died young, by their own hand or from the ravages of alcohol or drugs. Some were still hanging one but were pretty clearly damaged by their trauma.

I thought for example of Tom Holby – young Tommy, he was called as a boy chorister at St. Nick's. I didn't know him well back in those days, but his older sister was closer to my age and she had become a good friend over the years. She was a singer too – not allowed in the men and boys choir, of course, but she and I had sung together in various other choirs.

So I'd gotten to know Tommy a little bit and had watched him grow up. He'd never told anyone about his part in the tragedy, but the signs of its effects seemed to be there. He'd grown sullen and distant, even from his sister, she'd told me.

We'd talked about it a few times, she and I. She could never get her brother to open up to her, and I know it pained her that she didn't seem to be able to help him, despite her best efforts. And it pained me to see the sorrow in her own eyes, and to see her become – by extension, at least – in some ways yet another victim. As had so many others, in their various ways.

But the more direct victim, of course – it seemed obvious to us, even though he never admitted it openly – was Tommy himself. He had trouble in school, trouble holding a job once he'd graduated. Drank too much, got into drugs. In and out of detox and rehab. He'd get clean for a while, but then fall back into his old ways. I'd see him sometimes downtown, panhandling or just hanging around. One of Grayston's lost boys.

As Wolf and I walked, I tried again to clear my mind. Maybe I could tease out that nagging thought from the back of my brain. What the hell was it?

By now, Tom or the cops or someone would probably have told Hugh Parry, the minister, about Priya's death. If not, I guess I'd be the one. I'd have to talk with him about making some changes to the Sunday service. There'd likely be a proper funeral service later. But even for tomorrow I wanted to do something special for her. And the choir would too.

Nothing drastic, but it should be easy enough to switch the anthem for one of the Purcell funeral anthems. The choir knows those already. *Thou Knowest, Lord, the Secrets of Our Hearts.* That's the one. Priya loved Purcell. And for the closing hymn, *St. Clement – The Day Thou Gavest, Lord, Is Ended.*

An evening hymn for a morning service? I don't care. It was her favorite. Let them fire me. I'm used to it.

Wolf sometimes ran ahead, sometimes lagged behind if she caught scent of something. But pretty much she stuck close by. Good girl. Still, wary of hunters and knowing I had work to do back at the church, I knew we should turn back soon. I had promises to keep.

And miles to go before I sleep,
And miles to go before I sleep.

I turned back toward the cabin, calling and whistling for Wolf, who'd run ahead to explore something. She looked at me with a tiny husky whine of disappointment – she hoped we'd be up here all day – but back she came.

Getting ready to lock up, I made a routine check of the batteries in the flashlights to see if any of them needed charging or replacing. Something to buy when I was back in the city. One of the small flashlights was looking a little weak. I put it in my jacket pocket so I wouldn't forget to recharge the batteries when I got home. When you have no electricity, you don't want to be caught without flashlights.

Electricity.

That was it.

I swear one of those cartoon lightbulbs could have gone off over my head.

I locked the cabin, hustled Wolf into the jeep, started the engine and told the Bluetooth to dial a number. I had to talk to Tom.

Chapter 10

There be some that put their trust in their wealth
and boast themselves in the multitude of their riches.
— Ps. 49, v. 6

"Tom, it's Dugan."

"Hey, Mr. Heywood."

I don't think Tom has a cell, so I was lucky to catch him at home as he was washing up the breakfast dishes and finishing a coffee.

"Have you gone over yet to clean that vestibule?"

"No, sir. It's on my list. But I thought I'd tinker a bit with the boiler first. You know how she acts up in the cold."

That I know for sure. Old church boilers are notoriously fickle. And clanky. Just try recording music in the winter. Not worth the bother.

"That's OK, Tom. Go ahead and work on the boiler. But please don't clean the vestibule til I get there. It's important. I need to check something first. I'm driving back down from my land. I'll be there in an hour. Probably less. OK?"

"Sure, whatever you say. I'll see you when you get here."

Gotta love car phones. By this time, I was already off the gravel and onto the two-lane, winding blacktop that leads back south into Grayston. I was driving fast. Maybe too fast for these corners.

But now I was sure Tom would wait, I could afford to slow down a bit.

I wish I were driving my old Cooper. I'd make better

time. Most cars oversteer. The Mini understeers. Front-wheel drive, too short to fishtail anyway. And like the kayak, its centre of gravity is low, almost below the road. Sticks to the road like glue.

Still, my little Suzuki jeep was doing OK, making good time. At least it wasn't full winter. No snow, but getting colder. I was glad I'd already put on the winter tires for better grip. I passed Jeri's curve but was too preoccupied even to notice.

I made it back to St. Quentin's in record time, not even stopping at home to drop off the dog. It was cool enough, so I cracked the windows for some air and left her snoozing in the jeep. Husky fur against the cold. And no danger she'd be too hot.

I unlocked the door to the church hall, locked it up after myself and found Tom downstairs in the basement, adjusting something on the boiler with a hefty pipe wrench. You could do some damage with that wrench.

"Hey, Mr. Heywood. I left the vestibule alone, just like you asked."

"Thanks, Tom. I appreciate it. This may be nothing, but it's been bothering me and I'd like to figure it out. Can you please take me again through what happened last night, Friday night?"

Tom put the big wrench down on a table and wiped his hands with a rag.

"Sure," he said. "Like I told the police, Ms. Patel called and I let her into the building so she could practise upstairs."

"Why upstairs? Why not in the main room?"

"She always works upstairs. Says the old upright's easier to play than that big grand piano."

"That's true enough."

"And I think she didn't like singing all by herself in the big rehearsal room. Too loud. Besides, in this weather, the upstairs room's warmer."

That was true too.

"OK, so you let her in and locked up as you left. By around 10 you hadn't heard from her, so you came over to look. Was the door still locked?"

"Yessir, it was. And no alarm, so no one had gone out the fire exit."

"Were the lights on?"

"No," Tom said. "Not in the main hall when I came in. I turned one of those on. And not in the vestibule neither. I turned that one on and I saw her lying at the bottom of the stairs."

"And you hadn't heard her singing or running through something on the piano upstairs?"

"No. It was quiet. I mean, she might have been taking a break, or scribbling something on the music, I guess. Or listening on her headphones. She liked to do that too. But anyway it was quiet."

"And you're sure the vestibule light was off?"

"Sure I'm sure. There's a light switch by the door as you come in from the main hall. I turned that on, and there she was. Like I told the police."

"Yes, you did. And I think that may be important."

"How do you figure?"

"I'm not sure," I said. "It may be nothing, or it may be something. Let's go look."

We came up from the basement and into the main hall. There was more than enough daylight coming in through the windows. No need to turn on any lights.

The same in the vestibule, where the overhead light was off too, but plenty of light from the window. But there wouldn't have been much light at night, not in the little vestibule. Especially not in the rain. At night, you'd need the overhead light turned or you'd stumble around in the dark.

Because of the stairs going up to the upper room, the vestibule has a three-way light switch. The switch downstairs by the door controls the light overhead in the vestibule and also the light at the top of the stairs. The switch at the top of the stairs does the same, so you can turn the lights on or off without having to go all the way back up or down the stairs.

In the daytime, like now, the vestibule gets enough light that you don't usually have to turn on electric light at all. But if you go upstairs, where the windows are smaller, you'd want the overhead light – especially at night.

That's what had been bothering me, lurking in the back of my mind. Priya had been upstairs that night, surely with the light on in the office to be able to see her music and the piano keyboard. If she were finished and going downstairs to the ground floor, she wouldn't use the switch at the top and then go down the stairs in the dark. Too dangerous. She might trip and fall.

Which is what the cops think had happened.

But why would she do that? No. Much more likely she'd come down the stairs and turn the lights off at the door as she left the vestibule. She knew about the three-way switch. Had probably used it dozens of times. Even if the lights in the main hall were off – the hall had the same deal, with switches at either side of the room – at night there'd be enough light coming in through the big stained-glass windows from the streetlights outside that you could see at least well enough to cross the hall. Even at night, the lights in the main hall wouldn't have to be on. But the ones in the vestibule pretty much had to be. Especially if you were going up or down the stairs.

But assuming Tom was telling the truth – and why wouldn't he? – why were the lights off when he got there last night? Why would Priya have turned them off at the top of the stairs and risked not being able to see on the stairs on her way down?

It didn't make sense.

And it wasn't like her.

So assume she'd done the safe, sensible thing and left the lights on. If she'd done that, left the lights on but tripped anyway, fallen and hit her head and broken her neck – my heart cracked just to think about it – why were the lights off when Tom arrived?

Had someone else been there too? If so, who? And why?

I was talking Tom through his scenario as we got to the vestibule. He swore again the lights had been off. And it didn't make sense to him either.

"Humor me," I said. "Let's check the light switches."

Both switches worked just as they should. The switch downstairs by the door turned both the downstairs and upstairs lights on and off. The switch at the top of the stairs did the same.

So my theory was at least partly right. Maybe someone

else had been here Friday night and turned off the lights. Someone who'd seen Priya lying there and done nothing? That didn't seem right.

But maybe she hadn't tripped and fallen down the stairs. Maybe someone had pushed her.

"Tom, when was the last time you cleaned this vestibule?"

If Tom thought I was questioning his diligence, he didn't show it. But I think he knew me better than that.

"Well, I've kinda got a routine," he said. "Usually I clean the main hall and the cloakroom and this vestibule, and the floors in the kitchen, on Friday afternoons. That leaves me Saturday and early Sunday morning to do the sanctuary itself, so it's nice and clean for the Sunday morning services."

So he'd want to get at the vestibule soon, to clean up any mess the police had left. Otherwise he'd be even further behind schedule. I could see some fingerprint power on the handrail he'd want to be getting to.

"So you would have cleaned this on Friday afternoon, before Priya came?

"Yessir. I swept the floor here in the vestibule. And vacuumed the stairs and the strip of carpet. And wiped down the handrails. All on Friday afternoon. Did the main hall too, of course."

"Of course. OK," I said, "I promise I won't keep you much longer. I just want to look around."

"Sure. What are you looking for?"

"I wish I knew."

Tom went off back to his cranky boiler and his hefty pipe wrench, leaving me alone the small room.

We'd left the lights on after our little test with the switches. But even better, the clouds had cleared and some sun had been streaming in through the south window.

I was looking around but not seeing anything that inspired me or provided any answers. I went over and sat at the bottom of the stairs – which left me looking at the floor where Priya had lain. I tried not to picture her body lying there, lifeless. I wanted to remember her vibrant and alive.

Opposite the stairs, on the wall beside the door, was a small table. It didn't serve much of a purpose – sometimes it held leaflets or a decorative vase – but it was there in case it was needed for something. The sun shone through the window and from my lower vantage point on the stairs I thought I saw something glint in the sunlight. Standing up, I wouldn't have seen it.

I went over to the table, crouching down to get a better look. Remembering I had a flashlight in my pocket that still had some juice in the batteries, I shone it along the floorboard where I thought I'd seen the glint. Wedged in between the wall and one of the back legs of the little table, there it was.

A small brass button. Grabbing it by the little ring at the back, I picked it up carefully and looked more closely. It was embossed with a design of a little anchor and some braided rope. Not something from Priya.

But just the thing for a navy blazer at the yacht club.

Taking a small plastic bag out of my pocket – dog owners always have bags in their pockets for dog poop – I tucked the little brass button safely away for later.

Chapter 11

Shall not God search it out?
For he knoweth the very secrets of the heart.

— Ps. 44, v. 22

Sunday's service was subdued but beautiful. The choir members were of course shaken by the news of Priya's death. But they held it together and did her proud, singing their best.

On short notice, they did a fine job on the anthem I'd decided on – *Thou Knowest, Lord, the Secrets of Our Hearts,* from Purcell's funeral music. I played some instrumental music from that same set for the organ prelude and postlude. For his sermon, Hugh even used the text of one of the other Purcell funeral anthems, "in the midst of life, we are in death." And we closed with *The Day Thou Gavest.* I didn't think the music committee would complain.

All in all, a fitting tribute. Priya would be happy. Her family hadn't yet made plans for a proper funeral service. And they might or might not want the choir to sing. They might not even want a service at all. So for many of Priya's fellow choristers, this was their chance to say goodbye.

Coffee hour after the Sunday service was quieter than usual. Tom had cleaned up the vestibule – in fact the whole hall shone even more than usual. He'd swept and vacuumed and polished away any evidence of the crime scene tech. I'm sure many people by now knew Priya had been found in the small room off the main hall. But no one mentioned it directly. They talked around it, mostly small talk, though many had kind words to say about Priya and what a loss it was.

I thanked the minister for his sermon and he asked me to pass on his compliments to the choir for their singing. The wardens were there among the tea and coffee crowd, as they had been for the service. Philip Sanders came over to give me his condolences and ask if there was anything he could do to help. I thanked him and said I'd let him know if I thought of anything.

John ("call me Jack") Benson – it always struck me as odd that someone so stuffy and full of himself would go by Jack and not John, or even Jonathan – typically for him stood apart in a corner at the edge of the gathering, dressed in his expensive charcoal-grey suit and looking coolly over the room as if putting a price on everything and everyone. And deciding he was worth more than all of us combined.

After a moment he caught my eye and came striding over, a man always commanding whatever room he was in. At least he liked to think so.

"Dugan," he said. "Nice service."

His manner was smooth, though it didn't seem terribly sincere. I thanked him anyway.

"Of course, your choir isn't up to the standard I was used to at St. Nicholas. But at least you tried."

There didn't seem any polite way for me to respond. I managed a wan smile.

"Now is not the proper time, so soon after the death of – Ms. Patel, was it?" he said. "But I would like to speak with you at some point."

It was more a command than a request.

"As you know," Benson said, "the fundraising and planning for our atrium project are coming along nicely. We're hoping to have the funding fully in place, and construction to begin, this spring.

"So I think it would be good when we break ground, as it were, and begin the project for the church to have some sort of ceremony or event to mark the occasion. And of course we would have something much more grand when it's completed."

And when they put Benson's name on the dedication plaque, I thought. But I kept my mouth shut.

"So perhaps there could be some sort of musical element you could add to enhance the occasion."

Again, more of a command than a request.

Death was still in the air, had barely cleared the room, and yet Benson seemed more focused on money and improving the church and raising his own profile than on any more solemn or respectful concerns.

Odd. Though for him maybe not.

Of course I said I looked forward to speaking with him again at his convenience. I imagine I was barely more sincere about that than he was.

I got away as soon as politely possible and walked back to my place. I'd taken Wolf for a long walk first thing, so now it was my turn to get down to the lake. I stripped off my Sunday duds and put on my kayaking gear and not much later I was back out on the water.

I paddled out from my launching point and turned left toward the yacht club and the downtown area. But first I again passed the big construction project on the waterfront.

Until a few years ago, this whole area of a bit more than eight acres was a big, run-down open field – one of the last undeveloped parcels of waterfront land on this part of the lake and known by its designation on the city's official plan as Section J. Boring, hardly evocative, but a useful shorthand, especially for news stories. If you said Section J, everyone in Grayston knew what you were talking about.

A century ago it had been a small shipyard, then when that closed down during the Depression in the 1930s, there had been a succession of small factories and warehouses on the site into the '80s. But over the years as the old rail lines were lifted and as the surrounding residential neighborhood improved, the industries moved to new industrial parks on the outskirts of town. One by one, the old factory buildings on the site had been torn down or just fallen down on their own.

Amazingly, the one building that had survived had been there the longest. The old harbormaster's house. A simple one-and-a-half-storey frame cottage with a single dormer in the upstairs bedroom overlooking the water, the house had white clapboard siding, blue shutters and gingerbread trim along the eaves. It was a beautiful little cottage. Until the fire.

Now it was long since abandoned, charred from the blaze and starting to fall down. The doors and windows were boarded up but there was always at least one window where someone would tear off some boards to get in. Local kids on a dare or looking for thrills would sneak in to explore. Vagrant or homeless people would shack up there for a while, until someone complained and the police would swing by to clear them out. Every few months the *Gazette* would have a little brief – we sometimes call it a squib – about the old harbormaster's cottage and some incident there, most of them pretty harmless.

The heritage types had been fighting and mostly losing a battle with various developers over the years. Also the environmentalists, since it would take major remediation to remove industrial toxins from the soil. Most developers just wanted to tear down the cottage and get it out of the way so they could build their expensive condo towers. The historians wanted to preserve the old cottage as a little showcase. One developer a few years ago had offered to pick it up and move it somewhere. But no one could agree on a site and there was other legal wrangling, so the deal had fallen through at pretty much the same time that particular developer had run out of money and bailed.

So the city had swooped in. It sparked a huge fight at council but in the end council voted to put up the funds to buy the land from the bankrupt developer. Council turned around and sold some of the land to a new developer to get its money back – hence the first of two planned office/condo towers now in the works, remediation having been done. But in a compromise – and after another long, heated council debate – the little cottage and about an acre as part of the bigger parcel where the second tower would go had been severed off while the heritage types fought to preserve it. It had sat there lonely and forlorn, dwarfed and literally overshadowed by the new construction. Both sides were still fighting. Welcome to the politics of heritage versus progress, history versus big bucks.

But about two years ago a fire had pretty much made the whole thing moot. The fire marshal had investigated but couldn't conclude whether the fire had been deliberately set, a prank by kids that had gotten out of hand or possibly a vagrant's cooking stove that had gotten out of control.

The fire had damaged the old cottage almost beyond repair. None of that mattered to the unidentified vagrant whose charred body they'd later found in wreckage. Another John Doe for the morgue.

So now the debate was whether to restore what was left or rebuild a replica. Or just tear it all down and sell the land to the developer. That debate raged on and wouldn't be resolved anytime soon.

I turned and paddled away, staying parallel to the shore and not very far off. When the water's this cold, it was foolish to go out too deep. Most people would say it was already foolish to be out paddling in early November, but I like to push the season as long as I can. Still, I stayed close to shore. I may be foolish, but I don't have a death wish.

The water was cold, but there was a bit of sun and not much wind, so the lake was calm. It was an easy paddle and I wasn't pushing myself, just gliding along and enjoying the stillness and solitude.

That didn't last long. The sound of an outboard motor ripped through the quiet. To the east, by the yacht club moorings, I could see someone bombing around in a little black speedboat, doing tight turns and circles, playing in his own waves and wake. It looked like a 16-foot two-seater – not much longer overall than my kayak – but fitted with maybe a 60-horsepower Mercury, the big, black outboard easy to spot even from far away. A powerful motor for such a small boat. Built for speed and showing off. Or overcompensating. Not for cruising or fishing.

The noise cut across the water like a knife, tearing into the stillness and disturbing anyone within earshot. And soon it came buzzing my way at top speed. I didn't see much of the driver, half-standing at the steering wheel. Didn't look like he was wearing a life jacket. Idiot. Otherwise he was not much more than dark clothing and a shock of red hair that stood out against the pale grey sky.

Vivaldi's hair was so red, his nickname was "*il prete rosso*," the red priest. In other words, "Carrot Top."

And suddenly the noise was right upon me as the speedboat raced straight toward my tiny kayak. At the last minute, he swerved around me in a tight circle, jolting and nearly swamping me with the motorboat's powerful waves. The kayak rocked back and forth as I braced the water's surface with my paddle blades, struggling to stay upright.

I felt the little boat with its big motor circling me like a shark. I could see Carrot Top grinning like a fool.

Thankfully the roar and confusion didn't last long. After a few more spins, Carrot Top and his speedboat had made their macho point. Got his kicks out of scaring people, I guess.

Abruptly, he turned and headed back east toward the yacht club and beyond. I was happy to see him take his noisy, stupid, dangerous machine with him. As the waves settled around me, I turned and headed away in the other direction, to get far from the madding crowd and the maddening noise.

The jarring engine faded off into the distance, leaving me again on the quiet lake with my thoughts.

My thoughts were still a jumble. Missing Priya, remembering her laugh. Imagining her sprawled and injured at the foot of the stairs. Dying.

The thing with the light switch didn't make sense.

Had someone been there with her and turned it off later?

Who, why? Tom said the outside door had still been locked when he got there, the fire exit unused. No alarm set off. But the light was off. Why would Priya turn off the light at the top and walk down the stairs in the dark? It didn't add up.

I paddled a few more strokes, getting into a lazy rhythm. Dip. Pull. Wrist.

Dip. Pull. Wrist.

Tom could be lying. He could have come over, hit Priya on the head with that big pipe wrench from the boiler room and let her fall or pushed her down the stairs. Then lied to the cops about the whole thing.

Sure. But why? He had means and opportunity, I suppose. But motive? Hard to see it. And why call 911 right away?

Priya's boyfriend, Dev – had he been there and they'd gotten into a fight? Had Dev pushed her down the stairs? He was certainly big and strong enough to overpower her. Again, possible, but hard to imagine. Most couples fight at some point, but anytime I'd seen them together, they'd seemed fine. Not always an indication.

Come to think of it, Priya had made a passing reference to me that suggested there was sometimes some friction in their relationship.

I should talk to Dev.

Could there have been a random burglar? Maybe, but there didn't seem to be any signs of forced entry. Someone Priya knew knocked on the door and she'd let them in? Again, maybe. But how did that escalate into a deadly fight?

A churchgoer or someone else in the choir, another singer? Priya was the least like a prima donna you could imagine.

And I don't think we have any Mozart/Salieri-level rivalries in my choir. But I could be wrong.
Dip. Pull. Wrist.
Dip. Pull. Wrist.

And the button? Did that mean anything? Had it come off Priya's attacker in a struggle? Maybe. Or maybe it was already there that Friday night, had been there for days, even weeks. Wedged in against the wall, maybe even Tom's broom or vacuum hadn't picked it up. I saw it only by accident. It wasn't necessarily a clue.

And a clue to what? Priya's death was a tragedy, no question. Certainly for her family, for me and for others who cared for her. But that didn't necessarily make it a mystery. Sure, the light switch and the locked door didn't quite add up. And the brass button might mean something.

Or it might all mean nothing. Or nothing more than the initial police report: Priya had slipped or tripped or lost her balance and fallen down the stairs in the dark. Hit her head on the way down and broken her neck at the bottom.

Tragic. Deadly. But just an accident. An outward and visible sign of nothing more than a random universe messing with us again.

There is no God, only whatever order we ourselves can bring to the chaos. Or maybe there *is* a God, but he/she/God has no plan. Or isn't fully in control. Or doesn't actually like us much. Or has a mean streak.

Someone, can't remember who, said it's like three legs of a stool: God is all-powerful. God is all-knowing. God loves us and wants the best for us.

All fine and dandy, but it seems in the real world – the one we're stuck living in – you can only ever have two of those three at once. Not all three. Sometimes bad things happen because people are bad and they make them happen, or let them happen. Wars. Pollution. The Holocaust. Some people are starving because others are too greedy to feed them. Priests or choirmasters sexually abuse children while higher-ups look the other way and shuffle them around to cover it up. That's just humans being evil.

But sometimes, as another good book says, bad things happen to good people. People die in floods in one place while the country next door has a deadly drought. Good people die in earthquakes and tsunamis. A drunk driver crosses the centre line and sends your wife and daughter into the water to drown. Priya falls down some stairs and breaks her neck.

That kind of evil makes no sense. You can have only two legs of the three-legged stool: Either God is all-powerful and loves us, but not all-knowing, so can't see the bad stuff coming. Or God loves us and is all-knowing, but not powerful enough to stop the bad things from happening. Or God is indeed all-powerful and all-knowing, but sometimes just doesn't give a crap about us. There seems to be no other way to explain it.

Thomas Aquinas tried, saying God tolerates evil to exist so that some good may come from it. Sorry, Aquinas. Seems like weak sauce. Not buying it.

Theodicy, the theologians call it. Their attempt to justify why a benevolent God would allow evil to exist. From the Greek words *theos*, for god, and *dike* for justice. In other words, why is God sometimes just a dickhead? Irwin Shaw has a short story title that pretty much sums it up: *God Was Here, But He Left Early.*

Some people find comfort in thinking everything happens for a reason, that God has some master plan we're just not yet privy to. My wife's mother had a needlepoint that – fittingly – used needlepoint as a metaphor: On the face side was a verse with a lovely, orderly design. God's plan.

What you don't see is the underside – all those seemingly tangled but interconnected threads behind the scenes that go into making that lovely message on the front.

It's a nice metaphor – probably as good as any other – but I'm still not convinced. For that, I'd had to believe that God – all-knowing, all-powerful, all-loving – gave me a wonderful wife and child and then just decided one day to take them away? Why?

And was Blackwell taking my job from me – a job I loved and worked hard at – just corporate greed? Or was the hand of God at work there too? God wanted me out of the newspaper business to plunk me into a tiny church gig so that, what? I could find spiritual fulfilment? Discover that Priya's death was not an accident after all?

And forget about me. Why should God's plans in require so much suffering and death? Jeri, Chelsea, Priya – and so many others. Seems inefficient, not to mention needlessly cruel. What's that line from *King Lear*? "As flies to wanton boys are we to the gods. They kill us for their sport."

If I had to choose philosophers, I think Shakespeare has a better handle on it than Aquinas.

I paddled some more.
Dip. Pull. Wrist.
Dip. Pull. Wrist.

By this time, I'd paddled westward hugging the shoreline – no point risking going too far out where the water's colder and deeper, especially in case there might be other idiot motorboats around – past the hospital and toward the university campus. South from some of the student residences there's a large stretch of grass along the lake with a couple of odd, big, modern sculptures.

In warmer, better weather, the green space would be full of students playing with balls or frisbees, reading a book or just soaking up the sun. Today was a bit cold for that, too wet for sitting on the grass, but there were still a few people strolling around or taking in the view and of course a few walking their dogs. Which reminded me it was about time I got back to mine.

Paddling back on one side and forward on the other, I did a quick 180 and headed back toward home. But as I got nearer, I decided to keep paddling a little bit farther. The wind was light and the water still calm. There wouldn't be many good paddling days left before the ice started setting in.

So I passed my little boat ramp and kept paddling east, back toward the yacht club and the downtown core and the lift bridge. I wondered where Carrot Top had gotten to in his ridiculously overpowered speedboat.

I needn't have wondered. As I passed the yacht club on my left, I was pretty sure I saw him there. Odd. He didn't strike me as the sailing type. But there he was out on the open deck patio of the clubhouse – the deck chairs long since rearranged into a cluster chained together, where they'd stay until the club restaurant reopened the patio overlooking the water when the weather warmed up again.

Carrot Top was shouting at someone – or rather at someone who was just leaving the deck to return to the warmth of the dining hall inside. I couldn't see who it was. All I saw was the back of some guy in a dark suit retreating to safety. But that didn't stop Carrot Top from shouting at him, trying to get in the last word of an argument they must have been having.

Shouting. Arguing. Screaming almost. Waving his hands in the air. Carrot Top was obviously upset about something. The guy in the suit clearly wanted no part in this display, no desire to draw attention to himself. So he'd made a hasty exit.

Yacht club memberships were not cheap, and the club prided itself in being a classy, decorous place for a decent meal or a quiet drink. All the best people thought so. Some of its members didn't even bother owning a boat. They just went there to socialize. Be seen with the right people. Do lucrative business deals over cocktails and a handshake.

Paddling past, I was close enough that when he stopped shouting, Carrot Top turned and saw me out on the water catching the tail end of their heated exchange. Did he even know who I am? Some guy in a kayak. There aren't many of us. Probably the one he'd buzzed for kicks just a little earlier.

But beyond that, would he know who I am? Would he know how much I saw just then, or if I'd heard anything of what they'd been arguing about? Would he even care?

Never mind. Not my concern.

I kept paddling and soon passed the main part of downtown – the green spire of St. Nick's and the dome of city hall on my left. The *Gazette* and my own St. Q were there too, though I couldn't see them from my vantage point so low on the water.

When I reached the mouth of the river and the lift bridge that connects downtown Grayston to the urban township to its southeast, it was time to turn back. The lift bridge – which allows boats with sailing masts to travel upriver – has always been a bit of a bottleneck for vehicle traffic and there's long been talk of building a bridge with higher clearance farther upriver. But like many major projects – the whole Section J thing, for instance – the wrangling usually goes on for years before anything gets done.

I turned the kayak around and headed back. Picking up the pace, I got back to my docking point in good time, leaving me pleasantly winded. Not a bad idea to get the old heart rate up every once in a while.

Stowed the kayak around back of the building, quick shower, change, quick walk around the block for Wolf to do her business. It was time to talk to Dev.

Chapter 12

*My friends and my neighbors
did stand looking upon my trouble.*

– Ps. 38, v. 11

I know they were serious as a couple, but I was also pretty sure Priya had said they hadn't yet moved in together. They had different work schedules and each liked their privacy. I'd also gathered from a few things Priya had told me there was some tension between them about moving in together.

Which meant Dev still had his own place in a big old mock Tudor – "pseud-Tude" – place just off campus, not many blocks from mine. Wolf might have been a distraction for a conversation that was going to be serious and maybe not even easy. So I left her at home and walked over to Dev's.

My old reporter's instinct told me not to call him first to let him know I was coming. Maybe I was being too suspicious. But if he *was* involved in Priya's death, better to catch him off guard. If I could.

Dev Dhaliwal – medium height, muscular but trim – answered on my second knock.

"Hey, Dev."

"Hey, Dugan. Nice to see you. Sorry, the place is a mess. But would you like to come in?"

It wasn't really a mess. Just a small studio apartment, one of several in the big, old house, looking typical of a struggling grad student. Dev nodded to the small desk, with its laptop and a pile of books and papers.

"I was trying to distract myself by studying, but I can't really concentrate," he said with a shrug. "I've just made tea. Would you like some?"

"Sure. Thanks."

He went over to the small kitchenette and came back with a mug of Indian-style milky spiced chai. Not my usual, but when in Rome...

Moving a pile of books, he gestured me to the lone armchair. He sat on a small couch that I presume must pull out to become a bed.

"Thanks for the service this morning," he said, settling in. "It was beautiful – Priya would have loved it."

"I hope so," I said. "Nice of you to say. Everyone in the choir loved her. We'll all miss her."

"I know she thought highly of you," he said, "and she did love singing in that choir."

It was no big secret that Priya and I had briefly been an item. But if there was any residual jealousy or resentment in his tone, I wasn't catching it. He seemed sincere and genuinely the nice guy Priya had always said he was.

So why would I think he might have something to do with her death – with killing her, if that's what it was and not just an accident? Maybe because in cases of murder, as any good cop would tell you and as statistics seem to bear out, it's often the spouse or partner who's a legitimate prime suspect. Intimate partner. Or otherwise a business partner – but in Priya's case that didn't seem to apply.

But any good journalist would also tell you never to make assumptions. Just because the killer is often a spouse doesn't mean it's *always* the spouse. As biz prof Aaron Levenstein famously said: Statistics are like a bikini. What they reveal is suggestive, but what they conceal is vital.

So Priya may or may not have been killed, and Dev may or may not be the killer. As her boyfriend, he ticked one box, but as a person, he didn't seem the type. Sipping his chai and staring blankly at nothing, he seemed genuinely upset by her death. Of course, as Grayston well knew, some people are not always as innocent as they may seem.

Still, it would be good to know, just to be sure. I was trying to decide how and what to ask him, when he saved me the trouble.

"I just don't get it," he said. "It's so sudden. I can't believe she's gone."

Sometimes the best way to interview someone is not to say or ask anything. If they're talking, just let them talk.

"I saw her Friday morning before she went to work and I went to class. I'd slept over at her place – sometimes she stays here, but her place is nicer and closer to work for her.

"I feel really badly because we'd had a bit of a fight that morning."

"Really?"

"Yes, it's stupid. Nothing major."

Dev looked a bit embarrassed, but continued.

"It's funny, in a way, when you think about it. Rather the reverse of what you might expect."

"How's that?"

"Well, I'm not sure if you know. I know you and Priya are – were – still friends, but she may not have told you yet. We've been talking about getting married."

"No, she hadn't mentioned it."

"Well, we're not engaged or anything. It's been more a discussion about whether to move in together."

"And that's a problem?"

"Not for me. Not for either of us, really," Dev said. "It's my parents. They're very old-fashioned and traditional. They would not want us living together before we were married."

Priya and I were never serious enough when we were dating to talk of moving in together. But we'd had the discussion in abstract terms. I knew Priya felt she would want to live together with any man she was serious with before committing to marriage. So I assume she'd said as much to Dev.

"You didn't see her after that?"

"No. I don't know if you know, but I'm a TA – a teaching assistant – at the English department, just finishing my master's. And I've started taking a few courses toward a PhD – though who knows now if I'll ever finish it.

"On Friday night I finished my last class about 8:30. And I knew Priya was going to be practising anyway, so I went to the student pub with some of my classmates for a late supper and some drinks. You know – griping about professors and students how bad our workload is. The usual grad student TA stuff."

He smiled with a small shrug.

"Priya and I were going to get together again for breakfast on Saturday.

"I tried calling her before going into class, just to confirm a time for breakfast, but it went straight to voicemail.

"She still has that old flip phone" he said with a wan smile. "The battery sucks."

"So, when did you hear?"

"Not til late," he said. "I'd turned my own phone off for class and stupidly forgot to turn it on again. It wasn't until I got home, nearly midnight, that I noticed. I saw it was off when I took it out of my pocket.

"When I turned it on there was nothing from Priya. But there were a couple of messages from that Officer Kang. So I called him back. Helluva way to find out your girlfriend is dead. I didn't even know."

"I'm sorry," I said. "But there wasn't anything you could have done."

"Yeah, I know that," he said. "But it doesn't make it any easier to take."

"You're right. It doesn't." What else could I say?

"Listen," I said, getting up. "I don't want to take up any more of your time. I just wanted to tell you I'm sorry."

"Yes," Dev said. "Thanks. And please thank the choir for me. The music was perfect."

Walking back to my place gave me a few minutes to think. Something about Priya's death still didn't sit right. But if it was murder, her boyfriend was looking less and less likely as a possible suspect. It would seem Dev had a pretty solid alibi. If he even needed one.

I could go through the trouble of following up to check it, but that hardly seemed worth the effort. He was in a classroom full of students for a least a couple of hours, and had spent a couple of hours after that in a pub full of people until long after Priya died. Or was killed. Any number of people could vouch for that if I needed to find them.

There are security cameras all over campus, and certainly outside the pub entrance – there'd been enough vandalism and drunken brawls over the years that installing them had more than paid off.

So I was back to square one. If Priya had been killed – if it wasn't just an awful accident – I still had no idea who might have killed her. Or why.

Chapter 13

For man walketh as a vain shadow and disquieteth himself in vain.
He heapeth up riches and cannot tell who shall gather them.
— Ps. 39, v. 7

Dev's place, my place and the church form a sort of triangle, with the hypotenuse more or less cutting across the park. No rain, so I decided to check out a hunch.

Crossing the park to the church, I felt a bit guilty not having Wolf with me, promised myself I'd make it up to her later. Half the other dog owners might not recognize me without her in tow, just as I might not recognize many of them in a different context. Dog people tend to know the other dogs and their names, not so much the names of their owners.

At St. Quentin's, I checked the doors and windows to Macmillan Hall. No obvious signs of forced entry, as the police report probably said. Some tiny scratches around the keyhole itself – funny how we still say keyhole when modern locks have long since had a slit, not a hole – but to my untrained eye none looked recent.

Were there signs of the lock being picked? If there were, maybe Sherlock Holmes could tell, but I certainly couldn't. Who was I kidding? And besides, any decent burglar could probably pick a lock without leaving a mark. Maybe not as easily as they make it look in movies or TV, but probably without doing much damage.

For form's sake I checked all the other doors and windows too, both in the hall and the church itself. Nada.

But getting into the church wouldn't have done the killer – if there *were* a killer – any good anyway. Partly because the church sits on an odd triangle of land and partly because money was tight in the Depression when they added the hall, the two buildings aren't actually connected. They share a small courtyard.

It's lovely in the warm weather – people leave the service and stroll through a little courtyard garden to get to the hall for coffee and social time. Not so nice in the rain or cold – as plenty of parishioners and choristers have griped over the years, believe me. There are plans all drawn up and approved to build a glassed-in atrium walkway. All we need is the money.

That's probably why someone on the building committee thought to lure Jack Benson over and made him a warden. He's rich, he has rich developer friends, he's influential and ambitious. They probably told him if he could raise the funding, they'd name it after him. Give him a nice brass plaque and a ribbon-cutting. He'd like that. And if he got that done, they must have thought, maybe putting up with his smugness would even be worth it.

Personally, I doubt it.

I was no closer to an answer about Priya, assuming there was one to be found beyond random tragedy. Since I was here, I should probably get in some practising of my own. But I really wasn't in the mood. Right now, I felt more guilty about neglecting my dog than my music. So I left, walking the short arm of the triangle back home.

Since shortly after the death of my wife and child, "home" has been the Grandview, a grand old 19th-century mansion of red bricks, turrets, bay windows, mansard roof and gingerbread trim sitting across from one corner of the big city park, one street up (and with much less waterfront view, several real estate brackets down) from the waterfront and just a few blocks south of my church.

Built in the 1880s as a private home, by the 1920s it had become the Grandview Hotel. Originally almost as opulent as its name implied, through the '30s and '40s it had slid a few notches down the old social ladder, though it never fell into full-on seediness. By the '60s and over the next several decades, with most of its large rooms long since chopped up willy-nilly, it had morphed into an artsy, slightly funky collection of small rental apartments.

I'd lived there for a couple of years as a student and after graduation as a freelancer. The studio apartment was small and didn't have a proper kitchen, but the rent was cheap, it was close to campus in one direction and the newspaper in the other. And my fellow Grandview dwellers were a nice, offbeat bunch to hang out with. Flush with my first real salary, I'd moved to slightly bigger and more expensive digs when I landed my first full-time job at the newspaper.

If I'd been smarter back then, I'd have stayed put for a few more years and salted away my money. But as that great old journalist Irwin S. Cobb once said, "If writers were good businessmen, they'd have too much sense to be writers."

After Jeri and I got married, between my newspaper salary and her office job, we'd scraped together enough for a down payment on a small fixer-upper in what our agent had assured us was a "promising" neighborhood. The house needed work, but that was part of the fun. And it was an easy walk to work, in different directions, for each of us. There was a park nearby for the dog we knew we wanted to get, and maybe even for a child in a few years.

It was a good prospect, even a nice life for a while.

My heart wasn't really in the house after Jeri and Chelsea died. Everything reminded me too much of them and the life we'd started to build together. I needed a change, needed to move on. But I (we) had rescued Wolf by then – she was no longer a puppy but still young – and I worried about finding a rental place that would take a dog.

Luckily for me, by then the Grandview had spruced itself up into a respectable revamped condo building. So I sold the house and bought one of the units – a two-bedroom apartment on the ground floor (easier access for the dog) that ironically incorporated my old student studio apartment. It was a weird but not unpleasant combo of stepping back in time while also moving forward into a new phase of my life. Single again, as I'd mostly been as a student. As Twain said, history doesn't repeat itself, but often it rhymes.

Wolf was as always happy to see me when I came through the door. I'd wangled my way onto the condo board, mostly to ensure as owners we'd be allowed, at least within reason, to have pets. Not a big fan of committees – too much like Sayre's Law, which says, in effect, that academic infighting is vicious because the stakes are so small. But rank hath its privilege, as they say. And if putting up with a few boring meetings and some tedious bickering was the price of a few of us keeping our dogs or cats, I was more than willing to pay it.

So back I went to the park, this time with her in tow. If I bumped into any other dog owners, at least now they'd recognize me.

Chapter 14

Their idols are silver and gold,
even the work of their hands.

Ps. 115, v. 4

Monday morning after my usual – walk the dog, paddle the kayak (water definitely taking on a new chill), shower/shave/ breakfast – I was ready to face the day.

But not ready to let go of Priya. The loss of Priya. I could feel it – in my heart, my head, the pit of my stomach. Sadness, sure. But also a nagging feeling – call it an old reporter's instinct – that something still didn't sit right. Cops work on hunches too, so I thought I should check in with my police friend Don Patterson. Maybe he'd have some new information or ideas. The coroner's official report probably wouldn't be ready yet, but maybe there'd been a prelim examination.

Aside from the big lake and the fine old architecture, one advantage of living in a small place like Grayston, especially downtown: Nothing is very far away. The walk from my building to the downtown core – city hall, the stores on the main drag, the farmers' market in good weather, St. Nick's, even the old brick building that houses the *Gazette* – is only a few blocks. And only a few blocks past that is the main police station. The cop shop, journos call it.

I had no idea what shift Don Patterson might be working. Midnights, for all I knew, though he'd been at the church Friday night to respond to Tom's 911 call about Priya. But police shifts are even more erratic than newspaper ones, so he could as easily as not be there now on a Monday morning after a Friday night. Not much of a risk either way – the fresh air and exercise would do me good. Feeling only slightly guilty as always about not bringing Wolf, I decided just to walk over there without phoning first. Unlike Dev, I didn't feel the need to catch him unawares. If he wasn't there, no big deal. At least they might tell me when he would be.

And besides, I could swing by the paper, see if Sandra Novak or anyone else there had any new info.

The walk downtown didn't take long. It was still early for some of the stores to be open. The downtown was fighting a valiant but not entirely successful battle to ward off the chains, so the main drag is a mix of local shops and some of the usual big names. A few years ago, the longtime business owners had launched a "save our downtown, shop local" campaign, which the *Gazette* had gotten behind – and not just because selfishly it welcomed the boost in ad revenue.

This was back before Blackwell had swallowed up the paper and so many others. Not that Blackwell would ever turn down ad revenue either. But the old family owner/publisher was genuinely interested in preserving Grayston's character and heritage, in supporting local businesses because it was the right thing to do. Not just because it also helped line his own pockets. Blackwell would have sold his own mother for a quick buck. Assuming he even had one. Probably born out of some primordial ooze.

My luck held when I got to the cop shop. Not only was Don Patterson on duty, the sergeant at the front desk told me, but he was actually at his desk, not out driving around. After a quick call, the desk sergeant buzzed me through a locked door – even a small town like Grayston, it seems, has tighter security now – and into the main office area with directions on how to find him.

It was a big, open room much like a newsroom: Cops of various ages and ranks sat at rows of desks with assorted piles of paper, some tapping away at computer keyboards, some on the phone, some with phones ringing, about to be answered or let go to voicemail. Some were standing around in small groups of two or three, maybe discussing a case, maybe just some game or TV show. While still mostly white and male, there was a diversity of gender and ethnicity that spoke well of recent efforts to better reflect the communities they served. (To be fair, Grayston itself had a long way to go toward full diversity too.)

Layers of conversation overlapped into background noise. In one corner, the quiet chatter of a police radio scanner squawked calls and talkbacks and codes – just like the one we have in the newsroom by the photo desk, though increasingly replaced by a smartphone app, keeping an ear out for any new developments on the streets. It all made for the usual hum of activity and slightly constrained chaos.

"Dugan!"

I turned to see Patterson weaving his way through desks and bodies, making his way toward me.

"Good to see you," he said. "Here, come into this office, we can get away from some of this noise."

Along one wall of the large room were several small offices – just cubbyholes, really, with a desk and a couple of chairs, but with a door that shut to offer greater privacy, or at least a little less noise. Not too much privacy, though –

each had a large window looking back into the main room. These were not the closed interrogation rooms you see on the TV cop shows, with the one-way glass for sweating the suspect. But at least with the door closed we didn't have to talk above the din of the main room, which I could still see through the window. And at least this way I didn't feel like a suspect myself.

"Coffee?" Patterson asked as we sat down. "No, right, you drink tea. Would you like some?"

I shook my head.

"Good call. It's probably even worse than the coffee. There's a pot going in the kitchen, but we usually make an outside coffee run if we want anything decent."

Hmm. Maybe I should open a fast-food joint near the cop shop. Call it Stakeout Takeout.

"So what brings you here?" Patterson said. "What can I do for you?"

He'd had have guessed already, but I told him anyway.

"It's about Priya. I still think there's something that doesn't sit right. Not just that she's dead. It's tough, but I accept that. It's the how or why. Maybe even who."

Patterson looked at me a moment without speaking. Maybe trying to decide how seriously to take me. He opted for a middle ground.

"Look, Dugan, I've known you for a while, read your stories, seen you teach my kid. I know you're a good journalist and a good guy. I know you have good instincts when something doesn't feel right.

"Hell, we even worked together on that crap at St. Nicholas. The *Gazette* did a helluva job digging into that scandal. You helped break that story after chipping away at it for a while. And your reporting on that – the paper's reporting generally, the whole team – helped us send that bastard to prison. And a good thing, too."

It's probably bad form for a police officer, at least in any official capacity, to call anyone – even a convicted felon – a bastard. But Patterson had no superiors within earshot and anyway the door was closed. He knew I would neither be shocked nor care. And besides, he *was* a bastard. No quarrel from me. And that was putting it nicely.

"But look," he said. "With Priya, I think you're chasing a ghost. Or something. Seeing a scandal or conspiracy when there's nothing there."

Maybe I looked skeptical.

"Hey, don't glare at me," he said. "I'm not saying you're always making things up, or going off half-cocked. But in this case, because it's Priya and I know you cared about her, I think you're taking this too personally. You want a better answer, but there isn't one."

"So, shit happens."

"Exactly. Shit happens. Trust me, cops see it all the time. Try to make sense of the world, it'll let you down half the time.

"Personally, Dugan, I think you read too many mystery novels. I mean, hell, if you really think someone killed Priya, where were *you* on Friday night? You were home alone, just you and the dog, right?

"Not much of an alibi," the cop said. "Should I be worried you had something to do with it? Of course not! Don't be stupid."

As he was talking, I was only half-listening. Partly

because I knew he might be right. And partly because something through the glass had caught my eye. A flash of red in a sea of blue.

"What about the autopsy?" I asked. "Has there been time for one? Or will you let me know when it's done?"

Patterson shook his head.

"Dugan, there's not going to be an autopsy."

"No? Why not?"

"Family doesn't want one."

"Any particular reason? Religion? Tradition?"

"Coming from someone else," Patterson said, "that might sound a bit racist. From you, I know it's genuine curiosity."

"Of course not racism," I said. "But you'd think they'd want to know how or why she died."

"Obviously they do, Dugan. They just don't see the need for a full autopsy. Unlike you, they're satisfied Priya's death was just a tragic accident.

"Look," Patterson said, "as it happens, the coroner is an old friend of the Patel family. He was even their family doctor before he took the job. He's known them, including Priya, for years.

"I spoke with him briefly on Sunday as part of my report," Patterson said. "As a courtesy to them, he'd done a quick examination of her body on Saturday before the morgue released it to the funeral home. Nothing invasive. But you know him, he's not an idiot.

"He told me – and this will be in my report – that having examined her injuries, and absent any other findings to the contrary, he agrees with the paramedics and with our initial police investigation: She had injuries, including a blow to the forehead and a broken neck, consistent with a fall down the stairs. No other obvious signs of injury. Or, you know, foul play."

"But did she fall, or was she pushed?"

"Sure, she could have been pushed, I guess," Patterson said. "But unless you can show me any reason to think someone else was there with her, it's more likely to think she just fell."

All I had was a light switch in the wrong position and maybe a brass button. Not much to go on. I didn't like it. But he was probably right.

After a beat or two of silence, Patterson said: "What's that razor thing?"

"You mean Occam's razor?"

"That's the one," he said. "You're always talking about that. That monk who said the simplest solution is usually the right one."

I don't *always* talk about it, but I got his point. And to Patterson's credit, I don't know many other police officers who could quote, or at least allude to, the 14th-century English Franciscan friar William of Occam and his famous theological dictum. Comes from hanging around church musicians, I guess.

Out of the corner of my eye, again the distracting flash of red. I looked across the room to see an officer escorting a tall, lanky young man with a shock of red hair toward a desk and sitting him down. He didn't look like he was in cuffs, so probably not under arrest.

But he didn't look happy to be there.

Could he be the Carrot Top bombing around in the speedboat yesterday and shouting at the man in the suit at the yacht club? Maybe. Maybe not. But then again, in a town this small, how many tall, lanky guys with a shock of red hair could there be?

"Who's the redhead?" I asked.

"Oh, he's a real prize," Patterson said, looking across the room, seemingly glad to change the subject. "Barely 18 and already in and out of here more than a few times. Patrick Callahan his name is.

"Probably a juvey record too – not that I'd know without looking, and don't quote me. But he's already got an adult sheet, and you don't usually get that right away without some practice."

"What's he done?"

"Mostly minor stuff," Patterson said. "Attempted shoplifting, which he denied. Let him off with a warning, as I recall. Some trespassing down on Section J. Drunk in public, thrown out of a few bars for fighting. Bit of a hothead, I'd say. Chip on his shoulder about something.

"Some speeding tickets. Like I said. Mostly small-time stuff."

"Any burglary?" I asked. "Could he pick a lock?"

Patterson gave me a look.

"One burglary charge that didn't stick, I seem to recall. If you're asking if he could sneak his way into your church, I have no idea. Maybe he could. But if you're looking for some connection to Priya's death, I think that's a stretch. I think he's more your smash-and-grab kinda guy, not an expert lockpicker. And have you ever seen him around St. Quentin's?"

He shrugged.

"Some of the other cops know him better, have dealt with him longer than I have. Some of them even think he might be the one who set fire to the old harbormaster's cottage on Section J. But he would have been a juvey back then. And anyway, there's no proof. Some cops just have hunches. Like journalists."

"So why's he here now?"

Patterson sighed.

"You and I could do the old dance about his right to privacy versus the public's right to know. And we could go a few rounds of 'bad cop/good journalist.' But we know you'd probably win in the end. And I don't need the grief or the paperwork."

"I'm not a journalist anymore," I said, "just a lowly church musician. Maybe just a concerned citizen."

"Ya, right. We'll probably be putting out a press release soon anyway, so I might as well tell you. Not my case, but I heard some of the guys talking about it this morning.

"It looks like someone smashed a window at the yacht club last night. Broke in and made off with some trophies out of a display case, any other small valuables they could find lying around. My guess is they brought Callahan in for questioning, maybe sweat him a little. If he didn't do it, maybe he'll cough up who did."

"Why would anyone steal sailing trophies?" I asked. "How much could they be worth, really?"

"If he thought they were real silver he could melt down and pawn, probably a lot," Patterson said. "But since they're most likely just silver plate, essentially nothing. But at the risk of intellectual profiling, I'd say your average smash-and-grab thief would not be getting a call from Mensa anytime soon."

As Patterson talked, I looked again through the glass and

across the room. Callahan/Carrot Top was slumped in his chair, head down. The cop who'd brought him in was telling him something, maybe asking him questions.

Just then, Callahan looked up and over at me.

He looked right at me, recognition in his eyes, and gave a little smirk. More like a sneer. I probably just imagined it. How would he recognize me, or even know who I am? Why would he care?

It's not like I'm famous. But in a small town like Grayston, you do get to know a lot of names and faces, even if you never meet all of them. Back when I was writing concert or other reviews in the *Gazette,* they usually ran with what we call a muglogo (sometimes "head furniture") – my name and hedshot and a 'Review' label instead of just a regular byline. By that, readers were supposed to know I was writing opinion, not straight, factual news.

I'm not sure every reader understands the distinction, especially when I might have a review and a news story or two in the same day's paper, even the same section, sometimes even on the same page. The joys of smalltown publications. But at least the label and the muglogo with its hedshot give the editors some cover: "See? We're clearly showing you it's just Heywood's opinion. He can still be objective in his news stories." And of course I tried to be. Succeeded, mostly.

Maybe that's all it was: Carrot Top remembered me from my hedshot in the paper, or just passing me on the street. Or more likely he was the guy who tried to swamp me yesterday. It did look like he'd seen me after that from the yacht club deck. Or maybe he just recognized me as that loony guy who's out in a kayak almost every day until the lake freezes over.

Maybe the sneer was just his macho, 60-horsepower Merc looking down on my puny, paddled kayak. Like how bikers on Harleys sneer at electric scooters. Or drivers in their ridiculously big pickups and SUVs looked down – figuratively and literally – on my tiny Mini. For some people, it's all about size. Or pride. Or money. Or power. Or all of those.

I'd taken up enough of Don Patterson's time. I'm sure he'd agree. I thanked him and got up to leave. As we walked out the door, Carrot Top's cop was taking him into another room a few doors down. More questioning. The redhead gave me another sneer. I tried not to take it personally.

Probably sneers at everybody.

Chapter 15

Thou hast proved and visited mine heart in the night-season.
Thou hast tried me and shalt find no wickedness in me,
for I am utterly purposed that my mouth shall not offend.
— Ps. 17, v. 3

Leaving the cop shop, I thought I'd drop by the *Gazette* newsroom. Maybe my luck would hold and Sandra Novak would be on duty. I wanted to bounce some ideas off her.

The *Gazette* has been in the same spot since its founding more than a century ago, a fine old 19th-century brick building on a downtown street across from the market square at the back of the city hall. It gave local politicians and reporters access to each other within easy walking distance for either side. Assuming they were on speaking terms.

And next door, an institution I'd call even more important than either the paper or the city hall: Maggie's diner. The best greasy spoon in town. Scratch that. Best in the world. Might as well be, anyway. Cheap and cheerful, it offered a sort of neutral ground where journalists, city politicians and other workers, students and businesspeople – from retail wage slaves to the city's top lawyers – could grab a coffee or a meal and hang out. ("Breakfast All Day!" the old neon sign says, liver and onions a student special.) If the mayor or your local councillor was not at the city hall, chances were good you could corner them at Maggie's.

So before hitting the newsroom, I stuck my head in the diner to see if Sandra Novak was there. My luck held. She was at the till, just about to pay for a takeout coffee. Perfect.

"I'll spring for that coffee if you have a moment to sit and talk," I said, walking quickly to the front counter.

"Sure, moneybags," Sandra replied. "Wanna spring for a muffin too?"

"Deal."

I ordered a black tea for myself and muffins for each of us and found us a twofer booth along the side wall, away from the door and the chilly draft.

"So what's up?

Sandra took the lid off her coffee and was about to take a sip when our server arrived with the muffins and my tea – a mug and one of those tiny stainless-steel teapots – and a spare mug for Sandra's coffee. With a nod and without even asking, she politely took Sandra's paper coffee cup, deftly poured it into the spare china mug, set them down, smiled and walked away.

What can I tell you? Best greasy spoon in the world.

"Again, so what's up?"

"Well, first I wanted to thank you for the lovely obit you wrote for Priya. I'm sure her family appreciates it."

"Thanks. Nice of you to say. Never easy, those things, especially on deadline. But Mr. and Mrs. Patel were really nice. Obviously heartbroken at losing their daughter in such a tragic accident. But they held it together. Even gave me some pix to use. A lot of them were blurry old family photos, but the hedshot was the best of the bunch."

"I'm surprised you found even that one," I said. "Priya didn't much like having her picture taken."

"I'm not sure why," Sandra said, "for such a beautiful woman."

"Nice of you to say."

Sandra gave a wan smile and there was an awkward silence.

After a moment she broke it.

"Hey, what's that great story you like to tell about Maggie's?"

"You mean the really crowded Saturday breakfast where I found myself sharing a booth with a woman I didn't know? Said she was a dancer. Being on the arts desk at the time, I of course assumed she meant ballet or modern jazz."

Sandra smirked. She'd heard this one before.

"Oh poor, naive Dugan. What she meant was exotic."

"Yes, she was just passing through town, dancing at the Shipyards as part of the circuit."

Back in the day, even little Grayston had a strip club in a seedy waterfront hotel. Long gone now.

"And when she said she was waiting for her 'old man,' you thought she meant her father, not her boyfriend. Jeez, how old *are* you?"

"Mock me if you want," I said. "I have no comment."

"I'll admit that's a good story," Maggie said. "But that's not the one I mean, and you know it. I mean the one about the big night."

I knew the one she meant. Of course I knew. So I told it again.

Flash back to a little over five years ago. I was pulling a stint as night editor on the lobster shift, working midnight to 7 in the morning. It was definitely a mixed blessing. By the hard-fought union contract it was a shorter 7-hour shift with a tiny pay bump for the off-hours sked. And the work itself was interesting enough – reading the overnight news wires and websites for national and international stories, choosing which ones would interest Grayston readers for the late-morning first edition. Back when we still had a bigger paper and more than one edition. Thanks, Blackwell.

But the hours sucked and it was lonely work. Often when I came in at midnight, I might be the only one in the whole newsroom. Maybe a photog working late processing pictures. Or, like Sandra, a reporter finished off a late-breaking story. There wasn't even a staffer to update the web in the wee small hours of the morning.

A copy editor came in at 2 a.m. and together we'd edit the stories for the print edition, write the headlines and other stuff, choose the art and slot stories onto the inside pages. Anything I thought worthy of the front or page 3 – the biggest news stories that weren't local – I'd pitch to the news editor as part of my rundown at a little handover meeting when the dayside print and web shift came in.

Like I said, the work was interesting but the hours sucked. I was constantly sleep deprived and it was lonely with just the two of us – myself and the one copy editor – for most of the shift. If the copy editor was sick or on holidays, I might even be on my own.

Maggie's opens at 6 a.m., so most mornings even just to see other humans, I'd go down a little after that to pick up a tea for myself, a coffee for the copy editor and maybe a toasted egg sandwich for my breakfast. Or dinner. Or whatever meal it was I was eating at the end of a long night.

Except this one night. It was a Friday night shift for the Saturday paper. Usually one of the quieter nights, since much of the Saturday paper had feature stories and longer reads we'd worked on ahead of time during the week. So the Friday night shift was usually just a matter of filling a few pages with any fresh or late-breaking news.

But that night I came in and the whole newsroom was buzzing. Almost every reporter and editor had been pressed into service. Reporters were typing away or talking on the phone. Sometimes both at once. Newsroom phones and reporters' cellphones were ringing and only sometimes being answered, depending on what the call display said. Editors were hunched over screens, reading and scrolling. The local and region editor was busy consulting with the photo editor, obviously making choices for main and secondary art. There was a sense of simmering, controlled chaos.

For what story I didn't yet know.

I must have been standing there a little stunned when I heard my name.

"Heywood! Come see me!"

It was the editor-in-chief, Greg Adams. Not in his fancy office behind the glass but perched on the side of an empty newsroom desk. Not exactly shouting, but obviously it was important. I went over to see him.

A deceptive guy, our EIC. Not deceptive in the sense of dishonest – he had integrity down to his bones – but just someone you'd likely underestimate on first meeting. His hair was full but tousled, his suits always rumpled and his shoes scuffed. He spoke softly but, you'd soon learn, with quiet authority. And beneath that tousled hair was the brain of one of the sharpest journalists I've ever known.

"Hi," he said. "Glad you're here."

Like I had a choice.

With hardly a pause, he went on: "The rest of us are going

to be busy on a big story that will take all of the front and pages 2, 3 and 4 at least, as well as the editorial page, the city front and one or two inside local pages. Exactly how many pages, we'll figure out as we go.

"So we're going to have a smaller news hole for the national and international wires. Just a few inside pages around the ads. And I'm leaving them all to you. I'm also stealing your copy editor when she gets here because we'll need her to help out on the main stuff. Can you handle that?"

"Sure," I said. "No problem. You wanna tell me what's going on?

"Yes," he said. "We have the Gascoyne story."

"Jesus! Really? You've confirmed it?"

The editor-in-chief paused, looking solemn.

"Well, I'll tell you honestly we're taking a bit of a gamble. Or a leap of faith. But I think we've got the story solid enough to run it. And the publisher's backing me on this, thankfully. It looks like there's been a big coverup going on. How big we don't know yet, but we can't keep letting them get away with it. We have to get this story out into the light.

"You know we've been working quietly on this for a while," he said. "There have been rumors for a while of something bad going on at St. Nicholas, something to do with Gascoyne.

"You've been helping with some of that writing and editing yourself already," Greg said. "And I'm confident our other reporters have been doing their own digging too. But the big break came just late this afternoon. We have testimony from the parents of one of the victims. And their lawyer vouching for them.

"That, combined with all the research we've been doing on background, makes this story solid enough for print. We hope."

Waving her coffee mug to signal for a refill, Sandra interrupted me.

"OK, I know Gascoyne was the big story. And we can talk about that. But I want to know the Maggie's angle. I've heard tell of it, but I've never heard it from you directly.

"Sure," I said. "It's one of the few funny spots in this whole grim, sordid affair.

"First of all," I said, "you know there hasn't been an actual Maggie for years and years. She sold it long ago to the guy who still owns it now, George Papadakis."

"I sorta assumed that," she said, "since I see him behind the cash register all the time. Sometimes even in kitchen serving up orders."

"Right. I'm not sure he ever leaves. So it was usually George himself I'd see when I came down on those early morning shifts. He'd always ask me what was new in the world, and I'd tell him some little thing I'd just read off the wire – a minor earthquake or a big storm somewhere. Or what some foreign politician had just said. Or something. And I'd get my two drinks and maybe one or two sandwiches and be on my way."

"Except on the big night."

"Right, except that one night. Or very early morning."

I'd been working away on the wire stories – it was otherwise a slow news day – busy with my own editing and not involved that night in any of the Gascoyne stuff.

I'd overhear snatches of conversations here and there and from previous news meetings I had a general sense of what was about to break. But I had no idea at that time how big a scandal it was about to become.

About 4:30 in the morning, the editor-in-chief called us all together for a huddle in the newsroom.

"Listen up, everybody. This is a huge story and an important one," EIC Adams said in his low, measured tone. "And it's crucial we get it right. The publisher is taking a big risk and going way out on a limb on this.

"Frankly, so am I. So are all of you.

"When this story hits the streets, it's going to involve not just Gascoyne and his employer and those in his circle but also a lot of other important people in this town. People with power and influence and, yes, a lot of money.

"Many of them are our biggest core advertisers," the EIC said. "And some of them aren't going to like how these stories, and the ones that will follow, are going to make them look. They could well decide that instead of spending money on advertising, they'll spend that money on lawyers to sue us for defamation.

"But that's our job as journalists – to expose corruption where we find it. And believe me, I'm sorry to say I think we've found it here."

The newsroom fell silent. No one knew what to say. Of course we all believed in the ideal of crusading journalism. You know: Comforting the afflicted and afflicting the comfortable. That's why most of us got into this crazy business with its lousy hours and mediocre pay.

But it's one thing to believe the ideal and quite another to contemplate getting sued into bankruptcy and losing your job.

"OK, pep talk is over," the EIC said, grinning ruefully to lighten the mood. "But seriously, guys. We have to be on top of this. If by any chance Gascoyne has some idea this is coming, I'm pretty sure he'll try to find a judge to grant him an injunction to stop us publishing.

"So we're going to publish two hours earlier than usual. Which gives us less than four hours to put this edition to bed. If and when Gascoyne's lawyer shows up with an injunction, with any luck we'll have thousands of papers in trucks and on the streets and already in readers' hands.

"So here's the deal," he said. "There can be no leaks. From this point on, I don't want you answering any phones unless you know it's from one of your trusted sources. And no one goes down to Maggie's for coffee when it opens. I don't want any city councillors or lawyers or business owners catching on that we have way more staff on hand than usual.

"Dugan," he said, turning to me, "you can go down like you usually do. And you can pick up orders for the others. I guess we can risk that. Now get back to work, everybody. We have a paper to put out."

"Oh, I can just imagine what happened next," Sandra said.

"Pretty much," I said. "So, about 6:15 as usual I go down to Maggie's – which fortunately was pretty empty still. No bigwigs that I could see. And sure enough, there's George behind the front cash."

"'Morning, Senator,' he said to me. He called a lot of people Senator. No idea why. 'What's new in the world?'

"'Nothing much, George,' I said back. 'Pretty slow news day. Not much happening.'"

I paused.

"'OK, I'll need 14 coffees, please – six black, two with just sugar, one with just milk and the rest regular. Three teas – one black, two with milk and sugar. And I'll have five toasted egg sandwiches, two with bacon. One of those on white and the rest on brown. Oh, and a grilled cheese and bacon on brown. Thanks.'

"George just looked at me, deadpan. 'Slow news day, huh?' He smiled, but God love him, he kept his mouth shut. And you know how the rest played out."

"*That*," said Sandra, grinning, "is a *great* story. And you're right – one of the few bright spots in a pretty grim scandal."

And a scandal it was.

Chapter 16

The proud have had me exceedingly in derision
yet have I not shrinked from thy law.

– Ps. 119, v. 51

Julian Gascoyne had arrived in Grayston about 15 years ago. So about a decade before he was to become infamous.

The Reverend Canon Gregory Chandler, the chief priest at St. Nicholas, had hired Gascoyne from England with the promise of a bigger budget and bigger choir – and therefore a better salary and more prestige – than a young musician was likely to have found in some small provincial parish if he'd stayed back home.

A recent graduate of both London's Royal College of Music and the prestigious Royal School of Church Music, Julian Gascoyne (RCM, RSCM), fresh faced and full of energy, had taken the reins as choirmaster with enthusiasm. Persuasive and outwardly charming, he lured men and boys from some of Grayston's best and richest families – university professors, doctors, lawyers business owners and more importantly their young sons – to join and help build up what before had been only a small and ineffectual men and boys choir.

To be fair, there were also among the ranks some poor university students and other stray and capable choristers. On rare occasions I was asked in a last-minute panic to parachute in as a countertenor substitute. But I never sang there on a regular basis.

And it wasn't just for wealthy families, though they were

of course the most welcome. Any boy with a good treble voice is a rare jewel for such a choir. So if Gascoyne or one of his scouts heard of one, the boy's parents were quickly persuaded that he should join the choir. This was especially true in the case of struggling single parents. Money was soon found for travel costs if needed, or to buy the grey flannels and navy-blue blazer (each with its distinctive RSCM badge) that formed the choirboys' uniform. Which of course made the parents grateful for the choirmaster's patronage. The boys were, after all, getting a free but valuable musical education. And prestige of their own.

Over the next few years, the choir grew in size, stature and musicality, singing services, giving concerts and making recordings in the church. And Gascoyne quickly became a beloved and respected member of the St. Nicholas and wider Grayston community.

There was also a mixed choir, with women and girls singing the soprano and alto parts. But once the men and boys' choir became established, the canon and music director relegated the mixed choir to singing just one morning service each month at most. The men and boys sang all the important morning and evensong services and festivals and did the bulk of the concerts and recordings. Gascoyne paid little attention to the mixed choir, and soon hardly any at all. He fobbed off that responsibility to an assistant and lavished all his attention on the men and boys. Especially on the boys.

That should have been a warning sign.

But no one saw it. Or at least admitted to seeing it.

Looking back, it's clear there were other warning signs too. But there are none so blind as those who will not see.

And the honor and prestige of having a choir that was gaining renown not just in Grayston but in the wider world beyond blinded many to what should have been some obvious problems.

The Rev. Canon Chandler was among those problems. His boastfulness and preening about the choir – quite unseemly for a member of the clergy – did much to enhance its reputation. No matter if the roof needed upkeep or the soup kitchen had to scrounge for funding, somehow Chandler would easily find plenty of money from the collection plate to support Gascoyne's latest ambitious concert or recording project – even once for the choir to tour the U.K. – or just for brand-new cassocks and surplices for the men and boys. The mixed choir, of course, had to make do with their same old robes.

Other matters – more spiritual matters – should have taken precedence. But for the canon – behind his back people sometimes called him cannon for the amount he was shooting off his mouth – nothing was more important than preserving the stature and reputation of the choir. And by extension of St. Nicholas and himself.

Chandler's sense of prideful self-importance infused itself like incense into the other, lower clergy members. And into many of the church members too. Jack Benson was one of those, at the time a young lawyer just starting out with his own practice, learning to ingratiate himself with the city's rich and powerful. I'm sure the arrogance with which he now carried himself had its roots in those early years at St. Nicholas, chumming with Chandler, Gascoyne and a select few over post-evensong sherry in the canon's fancy manse.

Things went on like this for several years as the choir and church's reputation continued to grow, and Gascoyne's stature along with it. There were sometimes rumors of some impropriety – why was Gascoyne spending so much time with the boys, and particularly with some who seemed to be his favorites? But Gascoyne would just chuckle dismissively, his easy charm seeming to evaporate any suspicion as mere foolishness. And Chandler was always quick to come to his defence, downplaying any suggestion that anything might be wrong.

So when one of the choir parents asked that the church install a small window in the door to the choir room – so even if the door were closed, as often it was, you could see into the room – Chandler dismissing any idea of a safety concern. And Gascoyne nearly blew a gasket, insisting (stupidly, it seemed to me when I learned about it later) that a window might change the acoustics. Why anyone would take that seriously is beyond me. But such was Gascoyne's influence, propped up by Chandler, that of course no window was ever installed.

But Chandler's long since retired and Gascoyne's in prison. You can be sure there's a window there now. A big one. The new music director insisted on it.

In hindsight, we should have been more suspicious of it all. I certainly should have been more observant. I'm a trained journalist, for God's sake. I kick myself about that now, ashamed of my own gullibility.

I know I didn't *like* Gascoyne at all. Never had. Talented musician, sure. No question. And he got results. The choir had become excellent under his tenure. But I always found him way too smarmy and self-satisfied.

He was nice to me on those few occasions when I'd parachuted in. But that's the thing about narcissists: They're manipulative as hell, but they can pretend to be pleasant, even charming, if they think it will get them something they want. I was doing him a favor, helping out at the last minute. And besides, since I sometimes wrote music reviews, including of his concerts, I'm sure he felt he had to stay on my good side. I'll admit it's a conflict of interest, my sometimes singing in a choir I might later have to review. But that was one of the reasons I never made it a regular gig, just an occasional rescue mission. And as I've said before, those kinds of overlaps are hard to avoid in a small place like Grayston.

Sure, he was nice enough to me. But I just didn't like his manner as a choirmaster. Too volatile for my taste. Lively and encouraging one moment, but the next moment shouting and throwing a tantrum over a mere wrong note or missed entry. Showering praise on some boys and scorn and derision on others. Verbally abusive, for sure. It was only later we all found out he was being physically and even sexually abusive too.

Which is the big story the *Gazette* broke in that fateful Saturday early edition. Which got the police fully involved. Which encouraged more victims to come forward. Which led to charges, a trial, a conviction and a lengthy prison sentence for the choirmaster.

But not before so many innocent lives had been lost, or at least irrevocably harmed and changed.

If only we'd paid more attention earlier.

Chapter 17

We took sweet counsel together,
and walked in the house of God as friends.

Ps. 55, v. 15

"Sorry, Dugan," Sandra said, gesturing for another coffee refill. I was still nursing my tea, now lukewarm. "You said you wanted to talk to me and here I am making you dig up old war stories. What's on your mind?"

By now, Maggie's was starting to fill up with the early lunch crowd. Pretty soon we might feel obliged to give up our booth.

"Maybe nothing," I said. "But I'd appreciate your insight. There's just something about Priya's death that doesn't sit right."

"Well, sure," she said. "A young person full of promise, cut down in their prime by a tragic accident. That never makes any sense to me."

"I'm not talking metaphysics – though God knows that's a big mystery too," I said. "No, I mean there's something about the crime scene."

"Crime scene?" I could see the reporter in her perking up. "The cops said it was an accident."

"I know they did. But I'm not so sure."

"Why?"

"Just a hunch. Not much more than a gut feeling. But you're a reporter too. You know sometimes there's more to a story than meets the eye.

"So," I said, "I'd appreciate your opinion on this."

"OK. What have you got?"

"Not much. But I'll tell you."

So I told her what I had – which in the telling seemed pretty thin, even to me. The locked door. The light switch. The brass button.

The button reminded me of the yacht club, so I also told her about the break-in there and the stolen trophies. And my encounter at the cop shop with Carrot Top. I wasn't sure yet if they were connected, but there seemed to be at least a possible link.

"Yeah, I saw the press release from the cops about the yacht club break-in. One of the other reporters did a squib on it for a roundup of local briefs. It's on the website now and might make it into tomorrow's paper if there's room. We had a short quote from the yacht club commodore.

"He said it was so minor he might not even have bothered to report it, but the janitor had called the police as soon as he saw the broken window and before the commodore even got there.

"Oh, I think you know the commodore, by the way," Sandra said. "It's Jack Benson. He's at your church, isn't he?"

Well, *that* was interesting. Or was it? Was there something connecting Benson as the yacht club commodore to Carrot Top as the smash-and-grab thief there? That was assuming Carrot Top *was* the thief. Which we didn't know yet. But maybe the cops knew. If he'd confessed by now. I could check that.

Or maybe it was all a big nothing. Just Grayston being Grayston. A bunch of unconnected circles that just happen to overlap to make a Venn diagram – but one that doesn't mean anything.

There might be one way to find out.

"Hey, Sandra, can you do me a favor? Can you check the clippings files for anything on Carrot Top? His real name is Patrick Callahan. Double L. I think he's just turned 18. I don't know much else about him except he's had some run-ins with the cops already. Some of it as a juvenile."

"Clippings files? Jeez, you're dating yourself, Dugan. I'm pretty sure that's all digitized now. I can just look it up in the database. I don't have to go rooting around in that musty old clippings morgue in the basement."

"Great, that'll save your allergies."

"For the juvie stuff the courts would withhold his name," Sandra said. "But I might be able to infer a connection to any other names that *are* given in the court records. Lemme see what I can find. I'll text you if I find anything and I'll email you any files."

"Terrific," I said. "I'll owe you one. But this might all be nothing. I've already taken up too much of your time. Shouldn't you be getting back to work?"

"Are you kidding?" said Sandra. "This *is* work. If Priya's death wasn't an accident, that could be a big story. Or even if her death *was* an accident, maybe there's a little bit more to this yacht club break-in.

"I don't have any other stories on the go right now anyway. So I'm pretty sure I can convince the city desk to let me run with this for a day or two at least. I'll talk to the city editor let you know what she thinks."

"OK," I said. "I'd appreciate it if you didn't tell the desk anything about the Priya angle. It really may be nothing, and

I don't want to upset her parents for no reason. But you *could* tell the desk you're pursuing the yacht club thing."

"Sure, no problem. I get it."

With that she got up, ruffled my hair playfully and walked out the door. Not sure why she did that.

But I didn't mind.

Chapter 18

Set not up your horn on high
and speak not with a stiff neck.

– Ps. 75, v. 6

Chandler – the Rev. Canon Chandler, as he insisted everyone call him except in the least formal of situations – had retired from his position at St. Nicholas as the Gascoyne trial dragged on. Retired abruptly, some would point out.

Chandler had always proclaimed his innocence, insisting during the trial and ever afterwards that he'd never had any idea Gascoyne was doing anything even untoward, much less as heinous as abusing his choirboys.

Many didn't buy it. Chandler was in charge of the church and ran it like his personal fiefdom. He'd hired Gascoyne. Nurtured him. Championed him in town and to the world beyond. Indulged and financed his every whim. How could Chandler not have known? Or at least suspect something? And if so, why had he not done anything about it?

For many in town, including me when I came to be writing some of the followup stories after the initial big splash of that fateful Saturday edition, it made no sense. Sure, the choirmaster had fooled a lot of people. But it seemed unlikely that Chandler, who'd worked so closely with him, could have remained so clueless. But those of us who'd had any dealings with Chandler over the years knew he was not exactly an intellectual giant. Maybe he really was just that clueless.

After retiring, Chandler continued to attend St. Nicholas

services on a semi-regular basis as an ordinary member of the congregation. We even saw him sometimes at St. Quentin's. After the scandal, some congregants had left St. Nick's and transferred their allegiance to St. Q's. Sometimes Chandler would show up at our services, if only to keep in touch with some of his old crowd. I'm not sure how welcome they made him, since he was probably one of the reasons they'd left. But he was obviously trying to remain on civil terms.

And of course at the St. Quentin's post-service coffee hour, I'd often see Chandler off in a corner chatting privately with our warden Benson. Still chummy, though their interactions now were maybe a bit more reserved. I'd even seen them talking briefly at the Sunday service right after Priya's death. From my vantage point through the crowd and at the other side of the church hall, that exchange seemed downright frosty.

The Rev. Hugh Parry – no canon, just a regular foot soldier in the ranks of God's earthly army – has always stood in sharp contrast to Chandler. Where Chandler was proud, aloof, vainglorious and – many of us always suspected – cunning and devious, Hugh is warm, genial, self-effacing and kind. Also, unlike Chandler, a compassionate and insightful theologian. When I wasn't fussing about getting music organized for the rest of the service – looking over the anthem one last time or reviewing organ stops for the postlude – I found myself actually listening to Hugh's sermons. And staying awake. Something I had rarely managed to do when I myself was a boy or even a grownup in the choir stalls.

I'd seen Hugh briefly before the Sunday service for Priya

to give him a heads up on the musical changes and we'd exchanged condolences only briefly afterwards.

But we hadn't had a chance to really talk. So I phoned him Tuesday after I returned from my dog walk and morning paddle. No question, the lake was cooling down, though a freeze-over was probably still a month away.

Out of town at a conference/retreat since Friday morning, his cellphone turned off, Hugh had returned late Saturday evening from the event – it turned out the other warden, Philip Sanders, had been there with him – to a phone message from Det. Andy Silipo of the Grayston police. So he and Sanders had each found themselves that night in a short police interview.

"Det. Silipo asked me about Tom Pulaski," Hugh told me on the phone. "He wanted to know the 'nature' of their relationship.

"Dugan, why would he ask that? As far as I know, Tom is the sexton and Priya was in the choir. That's all. I'm sure they were on friendly terms – they're both friendly people. But I can't see anything other than that. Tom sometimes let her into the church to practise. But he does that for any choir member who might want to – and you know several other singers do too.

"Do they think Tom was negligent? Or somehow otherwise responsible for Priya's death? For killing her? I just don't see it."

"One of the other cops asked me the same thing, Hugh," I said. "Asked if I thought Tom and Priya might be having an affair. I told him that was foolish. I think it's just routine. Just covering the bases.

"As far as anyone knows," I said, "Tom was the last

person to see Priya alive. I guess that automatically makes him a suspect. Along with her boyfriend, I'm sure. That's just the way cops think. Maybe they think Tom secretly soaped the top step to make Priya slip and lose her balance. Then he cleaned it up before calling 911."

"But I thought they said it was likely just an accident," Hugh said.

"Oh, I think that's the conclusion they came to. And pretty quickly. I've heard off the record that's what the police report will say. But you know how the police work – they're naturally suspicious. What's Maslow's famous saying? 'When all you have is a hammer, you see every problem as a nail.'

"So I think the police just naturally think first in terms of crimes and suspects. And I guess Tom, being first on the scene, automatically becomes a likely suspect. And Dev Dhaliwal too – just because if someone is killed, it's so often by their spouse or partner."

"It's all just so awful," Hugh said.

"You should be grateful that you and Peter were out of town at that retreat," I said, trying for a joke to lighten the mood. "You've both got a solid alibi. Me? I was at home alone with my dog. I can't otherwise account for my whereabouts."

"On the night in question," Hugh said, catching on to my slightly morbid but mocking tone.

"Exactly."

I didn't bother Hugh with my own suspicions about Priya's death. I was probably just being foolish myself in having any. Seeing a crime where there wasn't one. Like Maslow with his hammer and nail.

"But seriously, Hugh," I said, getting sombre again, "thanks again for letting me change the service music at the last moment. That Purcell anthem was a favorite of Priya's. So was the closing hymn. It meant a lot to the choir – and to me personally – to be able to remember her in that way.

"And the fact that you chose a text Purcell also set for your sermon was a fitting coincidence."

"Not entirely coincidence, Dugan," Hugh said. "Both those texts come from the prayer book service for the dead. But I *do* remember Priya loved Purcell. So you and I are of a mind on that.

"As I said Sunday after the service but I'll say it again now," Hugh continued, "the choir did a lovely job. As they always do. But especially under those difficult circumstances. Priya was wonderful, and we'll all miss her."

"Yes, we will."

Chapter 19

Then are they glad, because they are at rest,
and so he bringeth them unto the haven where they would be.
– Ps. 107, v. 30

The next couple of days passed uneventfully, as days often do. Priya's family held a private funeral on Tuesday morning. No public service. No choir. I was glad we'd had a chance to sing for her at Sunday's service.

Tuesday afternoon the weather cooled. I dropped by briefly to pay my respects to Priya's parents. As with Priya herself, we'd stayed on friendly terms. But it was very much an intimate family gathering. Dev was there and I said hello to him. But I didn't stay long.

Wednesday it got even colder. More rain. So much that I didn't even go for a paddle. I'm hardy – but I'm no masochist. It was a day for reading by the fireplace. Might as well enjoy my semi-"retirement" while I can.

What's that old Simon & Garfunkel line? I have my books and my poetry to protect me. ... I am a rock, I am an island.

But Donne said no man is an island.

So who's right, S&G or Donne? Maybe neither. Maybe both. Or maybe Huey Lewis: All I want from tomorrow is to get it better than today.

Donne must have been the magic word, because my plan to spend the morning by the fire was disrupted in a pleasant way – by a call from my friend Bill Garner, whose church gig I was filling in for.

"Dugan," Bill said as I answered the phone. "I'm back in town for a few days. Why don't you come over to the department? We'll have coffee in my office."

"Sure. Be right over."

By "coffee," I knew Bill meant in this case coffee for him and mediocre tea for me – cafeteria and restaurant tea being almost universally mediocre regardless of the source. But what the hell, Bill had been off researching in London and I hadn't seen him in months. We were overdue for a visit and a stimulating literary discussion.

"So, how was London?" Lukewarm student cafeteria tea in hand, umbrella dripping in the corner, I settled into Bill's visitor chair.

"Surprisingly drier than here," Bill replied, a little sheepishly. "And warmer. I didn't have time to take in any West End shows, but I always love seeing the buskers at Covent Garden. And I thought of you and Sherlock as I passed Baker Street on my way to the British Library."

"Glad to see you managed to squeeze in some time for actual research."

Bill took my teasing with good grace.

"Believe me," he said, "it's getting harder and harder to find fresh ground that hasn't already been worked to death."

"Remind me again what you're working on?"

"You'll appreciate this," he said, "considering how much we both love the psalms, and considering my old and your new church job. I'm looking at literary influences in the psalms found in the *Book of Common Prayer* beginning with the 1552 first revision – the 1549 original edition *BCP*, you may or may not know, doesn't include the psalms.

I'm trying to figure out who did the translations from the original Hebrew, and which poets or writers might have been involved in flowering up the English versions."

"Is there much to go on?"

"Not a lot, sadly. There's a great story that's been around for years that Shakespeare – or one of his friends, Ben Jonson maybe – must have had a hand in the *King James Version*, since *Psalm 46* has the phrase "though the mountains shake" and later "he cutteth the spear in sunder."

"Interesting."

"Oh, it gets better: In the *KJV*, the 46th word from the start is "shake" and the 46th word from the end is "spear."

"Well, there you go."

"But wait, there's more! The *KJV* came out in 1611, so they would have been working on it in 1610. And in 1610, Shakespeare was 46 years old!"

"That's pretty cool."

"Yes, cool," Bill said. "Except it doesn't really add up. As your friend Sherlock might say, that's the danger of theorizing when one has insufficient data."

"How so?" My tea by this time was cold, but the conversation was warming up.

"Here's the thing," Bill said, lapsing slightly into his professorial mode. "First of all, according to most reasonable translations, the words "shake" and "spear" occur already in the original Hebrew text. So, no help there. The *BCP*, in my opinion, is actually more poetic than the *KJV*. And in theory the prayer book should add weight to the Shakespeare argument, since the *BCP Psalm 46* includes not only the phrase "though the mountains shake at the tempest of the same" but also "the nations make much ado and the kingdoms are moved."

"So why is that a problem?"

"It's a problem because the *KJV* doesn't say "tempest," it says "swelling." And instead of "much ado," it just says "the heathens raged.""

"So we're going backwards?"

"Exactly! Why would Shakespeare, or Jonson or someone trying to flatter him, *remove* what seem like references to his works?"

"That's a puzzle."

"Besides," Bill said, "because the *BCP* has slightly different – and I'd say more evocative – wording, in that version "spear" isn't the 46th word from the end, but the 48th. If you were Shakespeare or someone trying to flatter him, wouldn't make sure that stayed the same?

"On top of that, the dates don't line up. The first *BCP* to include psalms was published in 1552, with revisions in 1559, 1604 and 1662. They've been tweaking it since, but mostly now based on the 1662 version.

"But here's the thing: Shakespeare wasn't even born until 1564. There were already two versions of the *BCP* with psalms before he was even born. And Shakespeare didn't write his *Much Ado* until 1598 or so, *The Tempest* until 1610."

"What about some of the other contenders for being the 'real' Shakespeare?"

"You mean like Edward de Vere, the 17th Earl of Oxford? Nice try, but he's 1550 to 1604. He would have been only two years old when the 1552 *BCP* came out."

"That's too bad. I've always liked that story."

"So have I," Bill said. "Damned annoying when troublesome facts get in the way of a charming tale."

"Well, Bill, you know what Mark Twain said about the Bible: 'It is full of interest. It has noble poetry in it; and some clever fables; and some blood-drenched history; and some good morals; and a wealth of obscenity; and upwards of a thousand lies.'

"And on the whole I'd have to agree with Twain," I said. "Even an agnostic like me who has little or no faith, who questions the validity or even the honor of much of church teaching – who sometimes secretly wishes there were easy answers to fall back on – even *I* can find beauty and poetry and yes, even sometimes truth, in at least parts of what that old book contains. The psalms, for sure. At least they can give me something to hang on to in an uncertain world. You could do worse than looking there for wisdom."

"'O where shall wisdom be found?'" Bill said, quoting a favorite verse anthem we both knew. "And where is the place of understanding?"

"Exactly," I said. "But don't even get me *started* on how crazy the *Book of Job* is."

We lapsed into a companionable silence. I was enjoying our little literary discussion. It was a welcome distraction from my sorrow at missing Priya and from the dark thoughts and questions still swirling in my brain.

Maybe I should consider going back to school. Take some courses at the university. Spend my days in pleasantly abstruse intellectual pursuits. English lit maybe, or even theology. Hell, I could study Milton and Donne and cover both at once. Kill two birds with one stone. After what I've been through recently, the life of a student certainly had its appeal. And pulling the occasional all-nighter surely couldn't be as bad as working the night shift all the time.

But after a moment, Bill pierced the bubble of my academic fantasy and brought us back to the cold, hard present.

"Terrible shame about Priya," he said. "I just heard yesterday when I got back into town. I spoke to Dev Dhaliwal last night. They'd had the funeral yesterday morning. He mentioned you'd dropped by the house afterwards. He was grateful for that."

"I'm glad. How's he doing?"

"Pretty broken up, as you might imagine. I know him through Priya, of course, and the choir. But also he was a TA last semester for my senior-level course on the 16th- and 17th-century English poets. I'm not his thesis supervisor, but we've stayed in touch. His area is Anglo-Indian writers of the diaspora – Vikram Seth, Salman Rushdie, Arundhati Roy, that crowd – not exactly my field. But he knows the field well enough to be a great TA.

"He was telling me last night how guilty he feels. He admitted he and Priya had been arguing lately about living together."

"Yes, he mentioned that to me too."

"It's not even about them," Bill said. "It was the pressure he was feeling from his parents to make 'an honest woman' of her. They felt Dev and Priya living together would bring shame to the family. Or I gather Dev's father slightly more than his mother. But you know Priya – she was a smart, independent woman. She wasn't about to let them push her around, no matter how much she cared for Dev."

"How was Dev taking that?"

No point yet airing my suspicions with Bill, but I wondered if I needed to check Dev's alibi after all. Maybe he'd slipped away from the pub long enough to confront Priya at the church, and then gone back to his friends to cover his tracks?

"He said they'd had a 'heated discussion,' as he called it, on the Thursday night before she died," Bill said. "And the mood was a bit frosty on the Friday morning when they parted. So now he feels like a heel whose last words to his girlfriend were anything but loving and kind."

I filed that away for future reference, making a mental note to make some inquiries about Friday night at the student pub. Maybe I should ask Sandra for help – she's younger, so maybe students would open up better to her.

Returning home from my visit with Bill, I got a text and email from Sandra, updating me on what she'd found out about Carrot Top. It wasn't much. But I was glad for her efforts anyway.

Sandra's own police sources and database research confirmed what Don Patterson had already told me: Callahan's minor run-ins with the law as an adult – mostly bar fights, drunk and disorderly, a few speeding tickets. Came close to losing his driver's licence over those but seemed to have cleaned up his act lately. Was investigated a few times for burglaries but only one charge, thrown out on a technicality.

Here was an interesting detail Sandra noted from the court records: Callahan's defence lawyer on that one burglary charge was our very own Jack Benson. Why would an expensive, pinstripe-suited lawyer represent a penny ante smash-and-grab thief? Some lawyers will do free or low-cost legal aid work, but Benson didn't exactly strike me as the *pro bono* type. Probably it was just his turn for the court to appoint him. You know, the old "if you cannot afford an attorney…" Miranda spiel we hear on TV cop shows all the time.

Or maybe there *was* some sort of connection linking Callahan and Benson. Maybe Benson was the suit I'd seen Callahan arguing with on the yacht club deck. Benson was the commodore, after all. And often would have lunch there on a Sunday after church. But what would bring Benson together with Carrot Top? I guess Callahan keeps his macho speedboat there. The term "yacht club" was really a misnomer. The boats docked there are hardly yachts. Mostly small- and medium-sized sailboats. And some cruisers and smaller powerboats like Callahan's.

So if it *was* Benson on the deck, they were probably just arguing about Callahan's noisy powerboat. Sailors and powerboaters are notorious adversaries.

Digging further, Sandra had found another possible connection: Callahan had a younger brother, Neil, who'd been a choirboy at St. Nicholas in the Gascoyne years when Benson was a church member there. There was no evidence Patrick Callahan had ever sung in the choir, but his brother had been a chorister until Neil's death just a few months before the *Gazette* broke the abuse story. Sandra's email included the death notice the paper had run when Neil Callahan died "suddenly" – "survived by his loving mother and brother, Patrick." He was just 11 years old. Tragic.

Sandra's police sources also told her they thought Patrick

Callahan was a good prospect for the recent yacht club burglary – it fit his M.O. – but at the moment they had no hard evidence. An ID tech – probably the same one who had been at St. Quentin's – had lifted some fingerprints from a smashed display case for the missing trophies, but there was a backlog in the processing department.

The "processing department" consisted of one harried and already overworked criminalist who'd called in sick on Monday and was still off work. With no backup. So any prints from the scene of Priya's death were probably part of that backlog too. Welcome to the world of budget cuts and staff shortages.

Reaching farther back, the sources had also told Sandra their strong suspicion that Callahan was also good for the fire at the old harbormaster's cottage. Way off the record – since this involved Callahan's file as a juvenile offender – they noted he'd been caught on at least a couple of occasions trespassing in or around the cottage in the days leading up to the fire. Police suspected Callahan had been casing the site. They had no motive other than vandalism – the old house was just a shell, long since empty of anything worth stealing – and they figured he and/or others might have set the fire just as a prank. Or maybe even just by accident. Boys playing with matches hardly ever ends well.

But this was all mostly supposition. Carrot Top was never charged in the fire, even as a juvenile. There were just some notes in his file from officers who'd found him trespassing and had let him off with a warning. He would have been about 16 at the time.

I read over Sandra's email a few times to make sure I

hadn't missed anything. The connections were tenuous and the information sketchy and speculative. Not much to go on. But I hoped with some more digging, something might turn up. Like Wolf, I just had to sniff around some more to find what I wanted.

Chapter 20

He brought me also out of the horrible pit, out of the mire and clay,
and set my feet upon the rock and ordered my goings.

– Ps. 40, v. 2

Thursday morning I admitted to myself I'd been shirking my church duties. Quick dog walk and paddle, then up the street to St. Quentin's. Time to get my music organized for choir practice that night and spend some time at the organ. Those preludes and postludes won't play themselves.

Walking toward Macmillan Hall from behind, I saw something I hadn't noticed before. One of the basement windows was broken. Getting closer, I could see a pile of broken glass in the window well.

Odd. I was sure I'd checked the windows and doors the other day and hadn't noticed anything. You'd think I would have. Was that Saturday? Sunday? I'd lost track of time. So maybe I'd just missed seeing this from before. Priya's death had rattled me, for sure. Maybe I'd just missed it.

But even though I've been distracted, surely Tom would have noticed any damage as significant as this and repaired it. Probably he'd already ordered a replacement and was just waiting for delivery. Again, not the kind of thing he'd bother telling me about. He'd just go ahead and do it or get it done. That's the sexton's job. He might have to fight the wardens over the cost. But again, not my department.

I continued around past the emergency fire door and toward the main door of the hall itself.

As I did, once again a brief flash of red caught the corner of my eye. Color and movement. I turned my head just in time to see someone hurry up the street and disappear around the corner. Someone tall with red hair? Maybe. Or maybe just a red hat – it was getting cold enough for hat weather.

Was it Carrot Top scurrying away after trying to get into the church by breaking the basement window? Why would he do that? What would he gain?

Maybe I was just imagining things. The red car syndrome – if you're thinking of buying a red car, all of a sudden you start noticing red cars all over the place. Maybe it was just that, only with red hair. I was fixating on Carrot Top and so I imagined seeing him everywhere, whether it was real or not. That's probably it. Just my overactive imagination.

And looking at the keyhole on the door to the church hall, now there seemed to be many more scratches and damage around the opening than I remember seeing before. Was I losing my mind? I walked back around to the basement window.

It would be tight fit, but someone – a youth or even a slim adult – might be able to squeeze through that opening and gain access to the basement.

So *if* neither Tom nor I nor anyone else had noticed it before, and *if* some random vagrant or burglar had tried and failed to break the door lock (thus the scratches) and instead had broken the window and crawled through the opening into the basement, maybe *that* person was the one who'd pushed Priya down the stairs and killed her.

And that was *if* her death was anything except an accident. Which I seemed to be the only one thinking it was.

And *if* there'd been a burglary, wouldn't there be something missing? Or at least some sign of a burglar rooting around looking for valuables? As far as I knew, there was none of that.

A lot of *ifs*.

And here was another: What if Tom himself were the killer? I could still picture that hefty, deadly-looking pipe wrench in the basement. Enough to inflict a blow to the head. What if Tom had broken the window and scratched the lock to divert suspicion away from himself and toward some random vagrant or burglar? Some non-existent random vagrant or burglar. And away from Tom killing Priya. For no reason I could think of.

This was crazy. I've read too many detective novels. Now I was seeing killers and conspiracies and coverups everywhere.

And besides, that would still rely on me not noticing the damage until now. But then, why would I even be looking? Tom would have no reason to believe I'd be suspicious about Priya's death. At least not until Saturday when I found that button and figured out the inconsistency with the light switches. Or what I thought was an inconsistency, anyway.

But if Tom were the killer, would I be the first person he'd call? Well, after calling 911. Maybe to cover for himself. Maybe not. Maybe I'm just too confused to think straight.

I knew one solution. Just put all of it out of my mind. Distract myself from these disturbing thoughts with a little music therapy. And there's nothing more therapeutic than Bach.

Since I was at the main door anyway, I went into Macmillan Hall – being careful to relock the door after me

– and from there through the vestibule and another door to the exposed courtyard where the fundraisers hope one day to build the glassed-in atrium, then into the church sanctuary itself. Unlocking and relocking doors as I went.

The St. Quentin's organ is nothing fancy – just a small two-manual with pedals – but it has a sweet sound and it gets the job done. Taking off my jacket, I traded my outdoor waterproof shoes for my organ ones. Leather soles and pointy toes are not my usual choice of footwear, but for playing organ foot pedals they're just the thing.

First up I played through a few choruses from Handel's *Messiah*. The choir would be rehearsing those tonight. Christmas was looming and although we weren't ready to perform the full oratorio, we'd been preparing a few choruses – *And He Shall Purify*, *For Unto Us* and of course the ever-popular *Hallelujah* chorus – for a mini-concert in December.

Which reminded me: Priya, our star soprano, had planned to sing *And There Were Shepherds* and the other solo recitatives that lead up to the *Glory to God* chorus.

Sigh. I'd have to rethink that. Drop those little solos and just sing the chorus? Or assign them to another soprano? Other sopranos might want them. But no one could sing them as well as Priya. Another reason to mourn her loss.

Messiah sorted, I turned to the postlude – Bach's *"Little" Fugue in G minor*, a perfect gem of melody and counterpoint. Even as I began playing, some of the tension and stress of the past few days started melting away, carried off by Bach's elegant brilliance.

There's something about a fugue that's especially satisfying. A simple melody and counter-melody – subject and answer, layer upon layer, with those inner voices adding nuance and depth. It makes me feel, for a moment at least, that everything in the world could actually make sense – if only we could see it as clearly and as orderly as Bach did. *Messiah* is lovely, and has a few moments of genuine depth and beauty. But Handel can't hold a candle to Bach.

As someone once said, Handel is predictable – but Bach is inevitable.

Chapter 21

*Let us come before his presence with thanksgiving
and show ourselves glad in him with psalms.*

– Ps. 95, v. 2

Thursday evening was our first choir practice after Priya's death. We'd had the Sunday service – and the usual short rehearsal beforehand – but that wasn't the same.

That Sunday morning we were all still in shock at her death – to our varying degrees depending how well we knew her. So the formality of a church service – the structure, the ritual, the routine – had helped us navigate that, I think. Funerals are like that too for the grieving family and friends. Structure helps impose order on the chaos. Like a Bach fugue.

And for the choir, there was the added sense of professionalism, of an obligation to perform well, especially in public. Even if that public was only a few dozen people in the pews. Many of them were Priya's friends and family who might not otherwise attend St. Quentin's. Her parents and Dev, of course, were there, and I'd spoken briefly with them at coffee after the service. It was heartening to see them and they were more than welcome.

The regular Thursday rehearsal had its own kind of structure. But it was much more loose and relaxed. My choristers and I had had some time to process our grief. Still, the mood was subdued and sombre. There were small smiles and some hugs, but much less of the usual joking around and occasional clever quips that, though at times disruptive, also help with reducing tension and building choir rapport. Within reason, of course.

We ran through a few hymns to warm up and then spent some time on the psalm, always a good workout for both ensemble timing and blend. I was glad St. Quentin's had continued this venerable tradition from its Anglican roots. Anglican chant – even Episcopalians often still call it that – is a method for singing psalms in harmony. Its own little world with its own little rules. With enough practice, a choir should be able to get the rhythm and pacing, the cadence and flow, by intuition and without a conductor. In the rehearsal room, I'm at the piano playing the chant on the keyboard and can wave a hand now then as a signal. But during the service seated at the organ, mostly all I can do is nod if necessary. And hope for the best.

There's a particular beauty to the psalms – the simple melody and harmony of the chant, the beauty of the poetry and imagery, the pithy wisdom to be found throughout the verses. Useful too: The time it takes to chant *Psalm 51*, the *Miserere* text most famous in the bigger Allegri setting, at four minutes is just about perfect for steeping a pot of tea.

But as lovely and poetic and insightful as the psalms may be, I'm still in the "less is more" camp when it comes to singing them. I've known ministers who insist that whatever psalms the lectionary says should be sung on any given day – and it's all carefully laid out, believe me – all those psalms should be sung *in full*. Sometimes dozens of verses! Gimme a break. I say let's sing eight to 10 verses and call it a day.

Thankfully, Hugh's on my side on this one. Another reason I like working with him.

Similarly, as a longtime choral singer, I've never understood the rationale of spending (I say wasting) so much time on warming up a choir with scales and vowel exercises and blending routines. Those have their place, I suppose. But especially in a church choir with limited time and a large pile of music to work through each week, I'd much rather spend precious rehearsal time working on the actual repertoire than wasting a lot of time on a warmup. Do that at home before you arrive, is what I say.

As one of my basses is fond of saying, "Who needs a warmup? That's why God invented psalms."

Because of the last-minute switch for Priya, the anthem we'd already rehearsed for last week was now in good shape and ready to go with just a little touchup. Terrific. We ran through that just for safety and moved on to a couple of the *Messiah* choruses. And then it was time for a short break.

I still hadn't decided whether to drop Priya's solo recits or ask one of the other sopranos if they wanted to pick them up. I saw the two most likely prospects, Barb and Julia, standing together talking quietly. So I went over to say hello.

"Hi, Dugan," Barb said. "I was so sorry to hear about Priya."

"Yes," said Julia. "Isn't it sad? She was such a lovely girl. And so talented. Such a loss."

They seemed genuine, I thought. So much for any kind of Mozart/Salieri rivalry in the soprano section. Couldn't see it happening. They answered my next question even before I could ask it.

"We've talked about it, Dugan," Julia said, "and we think

you should drop the solos Priya was going to sing and the choir can just sing the chorus itself."

"Yes," Barb said. "No one else could sing those as well as Priya. We shouldn't even try."

"Well, thank you, ladies," I said. "That's very thoughtful of you."

The rest of the rehearsal went well. We ran through the rest of our *Messiah* selections, spending particular time working again on the fast running passages of *And He Shall Purify* and *For Unto Us* and ending with the rousing *Hallelujah* chorus. Normally that would put everyone in an upbeat mood.

But I still didn't feel ready to celebrate anything.

Chapter 22

Take me out of the mire, that I sink not.
O let me be delivered from them that hate me
and out of the deep waters.

– Ps. 69, v. 15

Friday morning – a week to the day after Priya's death – was the coldest day of the season so far. There was a chill in the air. And there would definitely be a chill in the water.

Still, I'd promised myself I'd paddle every day – or almost every day – until the lake froze over or the encroaching ice made it too difficult. Other people have their polar bear swims. I have my polar bear kayaking.

But I'm not a complete fool. Nor glutton for punishment. When it gets this cold I have a wetsuit and neoprene gloves to help keep me warm. And I stay reasonably close to shore in case I overturn. With luck – and practised skill – I'd be able to roll back up as quickly as possible to avoid being underwater for long. Worse than that would be failing to right myself after a roll and having to make what kayakers call a "wet exit."

Worse than *that* I didn't even want to contemplate.

So, early Friday morning even before sunup I'd taken Wolf for a quick walk so she could do her business. I suited up and carried kayak and gear down to my usual entry point at the boat ramp at the foot of the street around the corner from the Grandview.

The sun was just starting to peek above the horizon, reflecting off the glass of the first of the two planned condo towers rising out of Section J. At least the lucky owners there would have a fine view of the lake. Not so grand for the rest of us.

Slipping into the boat and paddling out of the slip, I soon reached open water. East or west?

I decided to paddle eastward into the rising sun – at this time of the morning at this time year it isn't so blinding – intending to paddle past the yacht club, past city hall and the downtown market square to the lift bridge. And then back home. That would be more than enough for such a cold morning. No point being a martyr.

It was a bit difficult to see clearly with the sun in my eyes. Forgot to bring sunglasses. But in the early morning quiet, I felt like I had the whole lake to myself. Wasn't really worried about bumping into anyone or anything.

As I got closer to the yacht club, a low rumble broke the morning stillness. A quiet burbling I couldn't quite identify. A few owners keep their boats docked and in the water year round, with a bubble machine to keep the ice away so they can live on board even through the winter. Beats paying market rent, I guess.

But this burbling didn't sound like that. And besides, it was too early for a bubble machine. There was no ice yet. This sounded more like a low, menacing growl. And then the growl became a loud, angry roar.

As a boat came out from beside one of the docks, I heard the sudden roar of a powerful motor. I saw a flash of black with a black outboard as the speedboat sideswiped my kayak with a huge wake, then quickly pivoted to return and bump me again on the same side. Standing at the wheel, I saw a lanky young man with a shock of red hair.

And then the shock of freezing water as my kayak overturned and I felt myself submerged upside down in the frigid lake.

Holy crap it was cold!

I knew I didn't have much time.

Thankfully, even underwater, I could hear Carrot Top's boat speeding away. Obviously it was Carrot Top. Who else would it be? I recognized the boat and the driver. Having submerged me, he wasn't going to stick around. He wanted to be far away, safe and dry, twiddling his thumbs and looking innocent when my body washed up on shore.

Had he really intended to kill me? To make it look like a drowning accident? Dugan Heywood, that idiot who goes out kayaking until the lake freezes over. Serves him right. Or did he just want to scare me? Scare me away from learning some secret? Or just scare me out of anger and for the hell of it?

All these thoughts flashed through my head in pretty much less time than it takes to say "flashed through my head." I was barely even thinking anyway as my survival instinct – and years of kayaking experience – took over.

Amazing how quickly you can get disoriented upside down in the water. Especially ice-cold water. Below your head is more water. Not good. Above the bottom of the boat is sky – and air to breathe. Makes no sense. But that's where you want to be.

If I'd been smart and wearing noseplugs, I'd have had lots more time – maybe more than a minute, depending how long I could hold my breath – to set myself up properly for a roll to return upright. If you don't have noseplugs, there's a trick some kayakers learn of creating an air bubble just inside your nose that keeps the water from coming in.

But I'd never mastered that trick. And I wasn't wearing noseplugs. So already I was losing precious time by having to expel air to keep the water out of my nose and keep myself from choking.

And God, the water was cold! I wouldn't last long in it.

I was glad I'd spent all those hours drilling the kayak roll, practising and practising until I could do it quickly and by instinct, almost without thinking. Letting training and muscle memory take over. But practising rolls in the nice warm summer water is a lot easier than in the cold. I was glad the wetsuit was keeping me warm – or warmish – but it was also adding bulk to the equation.

Reaching back and up to the surface – it still felt wrong, but I had to trust my training – and cocking my wrist to make sure one blade scraped the surface of the water at an angle, I swept the paddle around a half-circle arc while holding the tip of the blade at the other end. At the same time, I threw my weight onto the opposite hip as the kayak started to turn. The trick is not to throw too much weight or you'll just dunk yourself over onto the other side.

Thankfully that didn't happen.

In a mere moment, and grateful I hadn't completely run out of breath, I was once again upright in the water. Shivering, my heart racing. But upright. Freezing to death. But alive. More glad than ever for all those hours of practice. Not to mention the wetsuit and neoprene gloves.

No point sticking around. I was still freezing. I started paddling, as fast as I could manage, back to shore. Ditching the kayak and paddle where I landed, I ran home. I'd come back and get them later. If someone stole them in the meantime, boo-hoo for me. Getting home was more urgent.

I had to get into some warm, dry clothes. But first a hot shower. Then the clothes. Then a nice warm fire. And a hot mug of tea.

Maybe two.

Chapter 23

*But lo, thou requirest truth in the inward parts
and shalt make me to understand wisdom secretly.*

– Ps. 51, v. 6

James Bond famously takes a scalding-hot shower, then cuts the hot water back and back until he finishes with an icy-cold one.

Screw that. I'm no James Bond.

The hot water – as hot as I could manage it – felt great. Wasting no time, I hadn't even taken off the wetsuit at first. Peeled it off instead while I stood under the hot spray. And then stood there some more.

When I finally stopped shivering and felt human again, I dried off, got dressed in extra layers and made a big pot of strong black tea.

I called the cop shop and luckily was able to connect with Don Patterson right away. I filled him in on my little adventure with Carrot Top. Maybe now he'd take my suspicions more seriously.

"That *is* very interesting, Dugan," he said. "Your timing is good. Callahan is scheduled to appear before a judge in less than an hour. This might help our case. I'll speak with the prosecutor and tell them about this. I'll need you to come in later and make a formal statement. But for now I'd better get on this. Talk to you later."

I hadn't actually made a fire but was sitting by the fireplace with Wolf curled up on the rug by my feet. About halfway through my second mug and thinking a toasty fire might be just the thing, my cellphone rang. The caller ID showed a number I still have in my contacts.

Priya's mother.

Probably just phoning to thank me for dropping by after the funeral to offer my condolences.

"Hi, Mrs. Patel. How are you?"

"I'm fine, Dugan," she said. "Well, about as well as one can expect under the circumstances. It's hard, you know. But we're holding up."

"I know it's hard," I said. "We all miss Priya. Please let me know if there's anything I can do."

"Thank you for saying so. In fact, I think there is. I've found something odd and troubling. I could use your advice."

"I'd be happy to help any way I can. What do you need?"

"There's something I need to show you, Can you come by the house?"

"Of course. I'll see you shortly."

I had no idea what she would need to show me. What could Priya's mother have found that she'd find troubling?

Spiced chai tea twice in the same week is more than I usually have – the black-vs.-milky-chai question was an affectionate ongoing debate when Priya and I had been a couple – but Mrs. Patel had so graciously offered that of course I accepted.

Besides, I still needed warming up.

"Thank you so much for coming over, Dugan," Mrs. Patel said, pouring the chai from an elegant teapot that looked like a well-used family piece.

"My husband apologizes for not being here, but of course he's at work. We also wanted both to thank you for dropping by after Priya's funeral. And especially for being such a good friend to her over the years."

"Of course you're welcome. I was lucky to have her as my friend."

"You know she loved her singing and loved being in your choir. It always made her so happy. I'm glad you two were able to work things out and remain friends so she could keep doing that."

"I'm glad too."

"But my husband and I need your help. About Priya. We could go to the police, and maybe we should, but we respect your opinion and we'd like your advice first."

Police? About Priya? What was I missing?

As far as I knew, I was the only one who suspected Priya's death was anything other than an accident. And the only people I'd shared those suspicions with were my police and reporter friends. Certainly not with Priya's parents. Or anyone else.

"I'm sorry," I said. "I'm glad to help if I can. But I don't understand."

"Oh, of course not," Priya's mother said. "I should explain. We think Priya's death might not have been an accident after all."

Wow. Who knew? I must have looked stunned.

"I know this may come as a shock –"

Maybe less than you think, I thought.

"– but I found something that we think is very suspicious. Here, let me get it."

Mrs. Patel got up and went into the next room. After a moment she came back carrying a purse. It looked very much like Priya's purse that I'd last seen a week ago with her body as the paramedics were wheeling it away.

"The police gave Priya's purse back to us after we'd claimed her body. They had concluded her death was an accident. And of course at the time we had no reason to think otherwise.

"I was sorting through her things – you know, putting aside the identification in her wallet, a picture of Dev that we gave back to him. That old flip phone with its battery dead – she rarely remembered to keep it charged. Otherwise she might have called someone for help that night."

Called for help? That seemed an odd thing for Mrs. Patel to say.

"And then I found her MP3 player."

For such a progressive and enlightened woman, Priya was decidedly old school when it came to technology. The flip phone was one example – she'd never bothered to upgrade to even the simplest smartphone. The MP3 player/recorder was another.

"She used it for listening to music, of course," Mrs. Patel said. "She would download recordings or make her own – like those choruses of *Messiah*, for instance – so she could listen, and sometimes sing along, as a quick way of practising. Or just for enjoyment.

"And anytime I suggested she could get a newer cellphone that could also hold music, she'd say she was happy with her old MP3 device. Sometimes when she was practising on her own, she would record herself so she could listen back to it later as a way of looking for mistakes and improving.

"The nice thing about that for me," Mrs. Patel said, "and she was right about this, was that she would sometimes leave the MP3 player with me so I could listen to her sing. She knew I liked that. And that way, she still had the use of her phone."

"Yes, I remember she would do that," I said. "But I still don't understand how this could involve the police. Or what advice you need from me."

"We were so upset after she died, you understand. And when I found this in her purse, I thought it might have some recordings of her singing. And we so wanted to hear her lovely voice again."

"Yes, I can see how that would be a comfort."

"So last night – Thursday night was always her regular choir night, and she loved it so much, it seemed like the appropriate time – my husband and I turned on the MP3 player, hoping to hear our wonderful daughter sing again.

"What we heard was this. Here, let me play it for you."

Priya's mother pushed the Play button and placed the device on a small table beside the tea service.

What we heard began as the opening bars of *And He Shall Purify*, the first *Messiah* chorus the St. Quentin's choir would be singing at our little December concert. Priya must have recorded this at one of our own rehearsals. I could hear her voice – blending nicely, but distinctive and clear – in the choral mix.

I shot a puzzled glance at Mrs. Patel. She raised her hand slightly as if to say, *"Just wait."*

– And there it was. A few more bars and suddenly the music was gone. I could hear voices speaking. No, shouting. Two voices. Male. Angry.

And when I listened to what they were saying, I was shocked.

But a lot of things suddenly became more clear.

Chapter 24

O how sweet are thy words unto my throat,
yea, sweeter than honey unto my mouth!
– Ps. 119, v. 103

" – Just chop off his left arm, let him bleed into the gutter. Yeah, like that."

The things you hear in a newsroom that sound grisly from grizzled news veterans.

I came into the *Gazette* newsroom early Friday afternoon after my early morning near-death experience and then my meeting with Priya's mother. I had Priya's MP3 device in my pocket. And a backup copy of the audio on my own phone, just in case.

I was on my way to see Sandra. Walking by one of the workstations, I overheard that snatch of dialogue, just a designer telling a paginator how to play the art, cropping a photo on the full-screen display – the gutter being that narrow line of white space between the columns of print.

Funny how when it's just blank white paper we call it news*print*. But once there's actual ink and printing on it, we call it news*paper*. Go figure.

The language around newspapers has always fascinated me, even long before I got into the profession myself. I can remember even as a kid barely old enough to understand the comics – with jokes I was mostly still too young to get – lying on the floor with pages of the Saturday newspaper in front of me, looking at the pictures and stories, trying to sound out the words. Noticing that some of the words were printed much bigger than the others.

By osmosis most of us pick up an easy term like 'headline' because we hear other people – maybe news readers on radio or TV – say it. But it wasn't til I fell into the newspaper business myself that I learned some of the more abstruse terminology: 'Headline' becomes 'head.' 'Headshot' is related to 'headline' only in the sense that your head is on top of your body and the headline is on top of the story. A 'deck' is the smaller, secondary head. Some non-journalists might call that a 'subhead,' but for most journalists subheads are the small ones that appear in columns of type to denote sections of the story, or for a long story just to help break up the greyness of the page.

And of course journalists being lazy – and usually pressed for time on deadline – spelling scribbled in a note or now an email or message gets shortened. So head becomes hed and headshot becomes hedshot. Deck becomes dek and subhead becomes sub. Pictures on the page – often just called the 'art,' since the art might be a photo or a chart or something else – might just be 'pix.'

A paragraph is a graf and the opening graf of a story is the lede. Not lead, since that looks confusingly like lead as in a plumber's lead pipe. And in the old days before I got into the biz and before computer typesetting – I'm not *that* old, Sandra – type was cast in hot lead, set line by line and held together on a page-sized wooden form. Typesetters and editors learned the skill of reading type backwards, and often upside down, on the form – "on the stone" – before it got printed onto the page.

After a story ran, if there was more to tell, the reporter might write a '2nd-day' or 'follo' story, getting quotes from a 'streeter' (a more recent inclusive term than the old 'man-in-the-street' story). Sometimes writing a story or hed or designing a layout, we'd fill the space with 'TK' or even 'TKTKTK.' For something "to come" later. Not entirely sure why it's TK and not TC, except I think TK is a combination of letters you rarely if ever find in English, whereas TC might look like part of an actual word left there by mistake. Some sort of typo. That's one theory, anyway.

And that's not to mention other journalist shorthand like invu, revu, reaxn, elexn, correxn, (or just cxn) sted (for instead), sked (for schedule with a hard "ch," or otherwise it would be "shed" – which of course would just be silly). Stet, from the Latin for "let it stand," for marking a suggested change you reject, to stay with the original. And finally -30- for "the end" – an abbreviation with many possible explanations and origins that no one can agree on. And others I can't think of off the top of my head. (Pardon me, hed.)

All of which is to say I love the lingo of my biz. Doctors, lawyers, plumbers, cops, musicians – most professions and trades have their own jargon or argot too. So it's not like journos are unique in that. But it is the language of a business whose business is language. So I think that makes it special.

I admit I'm also biased.

But I do find it hilarious that kids these days (listen to me sounding like an old fart) with their text-speak – their LOL and IDK and BRB and LMAO – think somehow they've invented a faster way to write. Ha! Lemme file a few grafs on that and I'll set them straight. Though I will give them credit: The shorthands are handy.

Social media – Twitter and similar platforms – for all their faults (and there are many!) are full of shorthand. They've also been a boon for breaking news, among other things. Keeping people informed, bringing people together – though also causing divisions and tearing them apart. Reminds me a bit of reading the newswires in the old days, my old job as night editor, with flashes and alerts, followed by a fuller story. Stories would move on the wire in "takes" – small chunks. Kinda like social media threads now.

The other thing I find funny, speaking of language, is how slow we are to change it, despite pretty rapid changes in related areas, like social interactions or technology. Just ask any feminist how long it's taken for "Ms." to catch on. Still some pushback there. Old-school newspaper journalists still talk in terms of a "press release," though I think the younger ones more often use the broader term "media release" to include our colleagues in radio and TV. And now websites and podcasts too. (Though what, I ask you, is a podcast but just a radio or TV show gussied up in a new format?)

People – maybe just older ones – still point their index finger to their wrist to show time's a-wasting, even though fewer and fewer of us wear a wristwatch anymore. Our clocks are in our cellphones. Or they'll still make a little pen-on-paper gesture to signal for the restaurant bill.

News photogs still shoot pictures – though I've heard the D.C. papers, the *Washington Post* especially, have a strict rule to avoid saying, "I'm going to shoot the president." No, you are going to *photograph* the president. They're touchy about that in D.C. And even though pretty much everything is digital now, we still talk about "film" and "filming" and "taping." We sometimes say "video" now for the noun. But "vidding" hasn't made it into the language yet as a verb for digitally recording something. We'll probably get there in another generation or so. Progress takes time.

"Hey, Dugan. What's up?"

Sandra had seen me across the newsroom and was working her way over to intercept.

Like many (most? all?) newsrooms, the *Grayston Gazette* newsroom now showed, alas, only a shadow of its former glory. Even in my day just a few years ago, there were rows of desks and workstations staffed by reporters and copy editors, editors, photo editors, photogs, designers and paginators. The clatter of keyboards, the ringing of phones, the undertone of quiet conversations (and sometimes not-so-quiet questions shouted across the room: "How many M's in 'accommodate?'") filling the air with the sound of a team of people hard at work toward a single goal – meeting the next deadline.

But Blackwell had sucked most of the life out of this fine old newsroom, "downsized" more than half the staff, leaving behind only a skeleton crew bravely trying to keep up the good work. Would this tiny crew be up to the task of taking on another Gascoyne-sized scandal? Would Blackwell even be brave enough, like the *Gazette*'s former publisher, to risk ad revenue and subscriptions on such investigative journalism?

Guess we'd find out soon enough.

We found a desk – plenty of empty ones to choose from after all the cutbacks – and started comparing notes.

While I'd been with Priya's mother, Sandra had spent some time that morning and early afternoon with Don Patterson at the cop shop getting each other up to speed. She'd dealt with him before and I was able to convince them they could trust each other. This story was messy and we'd need the police on our side if we were going to break it open. And Don was already well versed in the Gascoyne saga – of which this latest development was really just a follo story.

I told Sandra about my kayaking incident with Carrot Top – which from Don she already knew but wanted more detail – and about finding Priya's MP3 device. I played her the evidence Priya's parents had found on it – and told her I had a copy on my cellphone as a backup.

It was pretty damning.

"Holy crap, Dugan!" Sandra said after hearing it. "That's awful. And it's gold. We'll have to play this for the editors. Lemme just tell you what Patterson has told me so far and then we'll go talk to them. This is getting way above my pay grade."

So Sandra filled me in.

Callahan – my old boating partner Carrot Top – had been arrested and arraigned that morning, Sandra told me via Don. Coincidentally after he'd tried to drown me. That part I already knew from speaking with Don. But Sandra had more info.

The yacht club break-and-enter charge was relatively minor. But this was not Callahan's first rodeo, nor his first appearance before this same judge – who even with that might have let him off on his own recognizance pending trial.

But then the court heard the police were considering

laying much more serious charges of accessory to murder. The police had finally cleared up the fingerprint backlog and had confirmed not only Callahan's fingerprint on the yacht club trophy case but also a partial print at St. Quentin's that possibly linked him to Priya as an accessory, if nothing else. Add aggravated assault or even attempted murder (swamping me in my kayak, though I admit we were laying it on a bit thick to call that attempted murder) and the judge decided to set bail quite high. It would likely be impossible for Callahan to meet it. That sent Callahan back to jail to consider his options.

Sitting alone in his cell, staring at the prospect of a serious prison sentence, it didn't take Callahan long to realize his best option was to cut a deal and spill the beans on the man who'd put him up to many of his crimes – certainly the more serious ones.

And that would be Jack Benson.

Chapter 25

*He hath graven and digged up a pit
and is fallen himself into the snare that he hath made.*
– Ps. 7, v. 16

Flash back three years or so. Benson was slowly building his law practice and Callahan aka Carrot Top was an up-and-coming juvenile delinquent of about age 15. Their paths were about to cross.

About two years before that – so about five years ago, just as the Gascoyne scandal was blowing up and the *Gazette* was uncovering the dark secret that would eventually send the St. Nicholas choirmaster to prison – Callahan's little brother, Neil, had died of a drug overdose. He'd just turned 11.

At the time, Neil and Patrick's single mother and everyone else assumed it was just a terrible accident. Once a happy, cheerful boy, Neil Callahan had become increasingly morose and withdrawn. He suddenly quit the church choir – which he'd always loved – but would give no reason. Not even to his older brother, and certainly not to his worried mother. His grades slipped and he was more and more often skipping school to hang out with a new crowd of buddies – some of Grayston's older teenage "bad boys."

From there Neil got into drinking, then using stronger and stronger pills and street drugs – whatever he could steal or get his hands on. Patrick, then 13 and certainly not the straightest arrow, had nevertheless always avoided drugs. He got his thrills instead from shoplifting, vandalism and minor

B&E scores. He didn't catch on right away, but eventually even he could see signs of Neil spiraling down and losing control. But whenever Patrick showed any concern, kid brother Neil would clam up and push him away.

So Neil's overdose, though tragic, was not entirely a shock. Everyone considered it just an accident. The police and coroner gave it only a cursory consideration and moved on. Troubled kid gets into drugs, dies. Happens too often – in good families and bad.

Still, no one had bothered to ask *why* Neil was troubled.

If only they had.

But Patrick knew. He'd found Neil's body one day coming home after school, their mother still at work. Neil had left a suicide note for Patrick alone. He said he was sorry for not confiding in his big brother about his troubles. But he was ashamed.

Typical of many sexual abuse victims, and against all reason and common sense, Neil had blamed not his abuser – not the choirmaster who had sexually assaulted him several times in that church choir room with no window in the door – but instead blamed himself. Neil was too young and too vulnerable to understand it was not in any way his own fault. He'd done nothing wrong.

Despite the shame he'd translated into guilt, and though he felt he couldn't tell his brother, Neil did have enough courage and sense to follow the advice he'd always been taught. He'd told an adult.

Too bad for him he'd picked the wrong one.

So young Neil went to one of the St. Nicholas parishioners,

whom since he was an important lawyer Neil assumed he could rely on. How was he to know his trust had been misplaced? Jack Benson had already known for some time that Gascoyne had been abusing the boys in the choir.

Some boys, but not others. Like most pedophiles, Gascoyne was both devious and cautious. He chose his victims carefully – often lonely boys with a single parent, or sometimes with parents he knew would soak up his charm and revel in the spotlight and accolades the successful choir was providing. The glare blinded them to the truth of what was going on.

But Gascoyne was not always careful, sometimes just lucky. Some of his victims, of course, had perfectly decent parents, single or otherwise, who were neither absent nor blinded by the choir's accomplishments. Their only fault, if it was one, lay in being too trusting, unable to conceive that such a vile monster could exist in such an amiable place.

As Neil later wrote in his suicide note to his brother, begging him never to reveal the secret that shamed him, Neil had told Benson about Gascoyne, about the abuse, sobbing quietly behind the closed door of a vestry room. But Benson would betray that moment of bravery. Of course he promised Neil he would look into it, would speak with Gascoyne, would make sure Gascoyne would no longer hurt him or anyone else ever again.

And of course Benson was lying. He did nothing.

So Gascoyne just kept on abusing choirboys, as he'd been doing for years and years, pretty much since his arrival in Grayston a decade before. His secret was safe. The likes of

Jack Benson and the Rev. Cannon Gregory Chandler would make sure of that.

This little irony would come out later, when the *Gazette* finally blew the lid off the scandal: St. Nicholas of Myra, the fourth-century bishop in Asia Minor whose name eventually gave us Santa Claus, is the patron saint of children. And of RSCM, the prestigious Royal School of Church Music, where Gascoyne had trained. Also – and Carrot Top would appreciate this – of repentant thieves.

Neil didn't know at the time that Chandler was part of this conspiracy of silence. Neither did anyone else. Except his co-conspirators, I guess. Neil knew only that he'd put his trust in Benson. And the lawyer had betrayed that trust.

Some of us at the *Gazette* would later come to suspect that others at St. Nicholas church besides Gascoyne – members of the clergy, the wardens or other administrators – must have known or at least had their suspicions about the choirmaster's behavior. But they certainly never told us.

Eventually, toward the end – toward the beginning of Gascoyne's downfall – there began to be rumors floating around town that the church had some big secret, that something bad was happening. And I and various other *Gazette* reporters had dug around a bit and quietly asked a few questions here or there.

But you have to be discreet because protecting a reputation is a two-way street. Or a double-edged sword. Or something. The point is you don't just barge around asking leading questions, hoping to uncover embezzlement or abuse or fraud or whatever wickedness you think might be going on.

If you turn out to be right and there *is* wickedness to

be found – well, good for you. That's good investigative journalism. Bravo. But if you're wrong, you may ruin the reputation not only of the person or institution you're probing, but also the reputation of the newspaper itself. So you want to be careful with what questions you're asking and of whom you're asking them.

The point is that until that fateful night – the long night of Maggie's and the many coffees when a victim's parents bravely had come forward to confirm the rumors – few outside Gascoyne's inner circle, and of course his victims, knew the dark secret that St. Nicholas church had been hiding.

Patrick Callahan knew. But he would abide by his brother's dying request not to tell anyone. Not even when he encountered Benson.

By age 15 or so, Callahan was an old hand at minor break-ins and burglaries. Nothing sophisticated – he tried but never learned how to pick a lock. He relied more often on dumb luck. You'd be surprised how many people might lock the front door but leave a side or back door unlocked. Or he'd just smash a window or glass pane in a back door, hoping – and often he was right – that even if the homeowner had a burglar alarm they hadn't bothered to set it.

He was too young to have any connections to a fence – even quaint little Grayston has one or two, as my cop friends could tell you – but he'd grab any cash that was lying around and pilfer any other small things that caught his fancy. Videogames, consoles, laptops, cellphones, watches, bits of jewelry. Stuff he could keep for himself or maybe sell to his friends at school.

All of this background Callahan had told Don Patterson in an interview room at the cop shop after the judge had set bail and returned him to his jail cell.

So one night, Callahan told Patterson, he'd broken into one of Grayston's fancy grey stone houses, thinking it was empty. Fate had other ideas.

The fancy house belonged to one Jack Benson, rising Grayston lawyer and – though Callahan had not yet made the connection to his brother – still at that time a respected, if not respectable, church member at St. Nicholas.

Caught in the act, Callahan's future was in Benson's hands. And the ambitious lawyer, sensing an opportunity, swung a deal. Instead of calling the police to report the crime, Benson recruited Callahan to be his personal burglar on call. Was it extortion or blackmail? I'd let the courts decide. Whatever it was, Benson had a hold over Callahan. And was prepared to exploit it.

If Benson needed information to help a case – dirt on the opposing side in a lawsuit or maybe a peek into a company's financials – Callahan could sometimes help him get it by breaking into the opposing lawyer's files or a company's office.

We're not talking sophisticated here. Callahan was hardly a master hacker, but like many teens he was pretty good with computers. If he couldn't find printouts lying around, he could sometimes break into computer files. Like unlocked doors, you'd be surprised (or maybe you wouldn't) how many people leave passwords written down and easy to find. If not, Callahan might just steal the whole laptop and bring it back to Benson. The lawyer had others on the payroll who could hack their way in if needed.

Soon Benson's legal career started really taking off. Bigger cases, richer clients. He gained a reputation as a savvy legal eagle. Mostly undeserved, since he was cheating. But still, it worked. He became the lawyer in town you'd hire if you wanted to win your case. The sheen helped get him elected to city council. Pro-business, pro-"progress." Benson became the darling of big developers and the bane of the heritage set.

Especially when it came to Section J and the big fight over whether to preserve the old harbormaster's cottage. Many on council wanted to block the Section J condo towers and preserve the old clapboard cottage. But not Benson – who despite an obvious conflict of interest (he just ignored the ethics commissioner on this) represented the developer who wanted to bulldoze it as part of the tower project.

Callahan by this time had somehow realized Benson was the St. Nicholas member who'd betrayed his little brother's confidence. But he kept that knowledge to himself. Benson could still send him to the police at any time for the burglaries he'd committed. Sure, Benson had told him to do them. But who'd believe the word of a petty thief against that of a prominent lawyer and city councillor?

Benson didn't pay Callahan, but part of their deal was that Callahan could keep whatever cash or anything else he found, since it made the break-in look more random and unconnected to the lawyer himself. So Callahan kept his mouth shut, bided his time and took the profits.

Until the fire.

Chapter 26

*He breaketh the bow and snappeth the spear in sunder
and burneth the chariots in the fire.*

– Ps. 46, v. 10

The harbormaster's little cottage had been the subject of long council debates, occasional grassroots pickets and even one hippie-style sit-in protest. The fight over its future had pitted local politicians, developers, preservationists, environmentalists and ordinary citizens against each other in a rancorous and drawn-out battle that had been dragging on for years.

And in mere moments, that battle was lost.

The quaint wooden 19th-century gem had gone up in flames one warm summer night – really, about 3 in the morning – and been consumed in less than an hour. By the time anyone noticed the smoke and the firefighters got there, it was already a lost cause. They easily doused the flames before the fire could spread and do any other damage, but there was hardly anything of the charred remains left worth saving.

All that fighting, all that passion on all sides, just turned to ashes.

It was only after putting out the fire and entering the wreckage that firefighters discovered the body in the rubble. Whether one of Grayston's local homeless or a passing vagrant, police and fire officials were never able to determine. They never identified the body, later buried at city expense in a local cemetery.

The fire marshal was likewise unable to determine for sure whether the fire was an accident or had deliberately been set. It seemed most likely the vagrant had rigged up a makeshift cookstove that had gotten out of control. Clearly he'd been living there for a few days at least. So absent any other evidence, the official report was that the fire was accidental. Heritage activists who disagreed talked darkly of conspiracy and coverup, even a bribe to the fire investigator – maybe the Gascoyne scandal had whetted the appetite for that kind of thinking – but nothing came of their protests.

They were angry but the developer was happy. He made a lowball offer to take that section of land off the city's hands and most everybody else just wanted to move on to other battles.

Jack Benson was especially keen to move on and, representing the developer even though as a councillor he also represented the taxpayers, he quickly pushed through a deal to offload the last remaining parcel of Section J.

Benson had good reason to want to put the fire behind him. He'd been responsible for setting it.

Not personally, of course. He'd gotten Callahan to do that for him. A favor – well, more of a payoff – for the developer, tired of having his expensive project delayed by "whiners and do-gooders." His words when he told Benson to solve the problem for him.

So, Callahan later confessed to police, on Benson's orders he'd gone inside with some matches and a can of BBQ fluid intending to use that to set the fire. The makeshift cookstove made it even easier to make the blaze look like someone else's accident. The main floor was empty. How was he to know the vagrant was sleeping upstairs in the bedroom? He hadn't bothered to check.

When the *Gazette* reported there was a body found in the fire wreckage, Callahan felt both panic and weirdly a kind of relief. He felt sick that he'd caused someone's death, and afraid of getting caught and sent to jail. But on the other hand he knew if he could keep this secret – what was one more secret to keep? – it also gave him more leverage over Benson. If police could charge Callahan in the death, he could take Benson down with him.

Meantime, he would use that leverage. He'd be a fool not to.

Callahan turned the tables and started extorting Benson. The way he figured it, they were both equally guilty. In fact Callahan, being a minor, suddenly realized he was in the stronger position. Big, rich, important Benson had much more to lose. And Callahan could always claim he was just a poor, misguided youth taken advantage of by the powerful and intimidating adult.

So Callahan's shakedown began. He still did small B&E jobs for Benson – they were easy and kept him in trinkets – but now Benson was also regularly paying him hush money. Then like most extortioners, Callahan got more and more greedy. Once he turned 18 and could no longer claim the innocence of being a minor, Callahan's demands increased.

That, Callahan told police, was what had brought him to St. Quentin's that Friday night – the night that led to Priya Patel's death. Callahan told Benson he wanted a meeting to "discuss the terms of their business arrangement" – in other words to demand more money for his silence. Benson by this time had left St. Nicholas (the better to put some distance between himself and the scandal) and been lured as warden to St. Quentin's, enticed by the prospect of his name on a plaque of that yet-unbuilt atrium.

Benson didn't want to risk meeting Callahan in public. Not at Maggie's diner, for instance, or even at his office. Checking the schedule online, he saw that no groups had booked St. Quentin's that night, so he suggested they meet there as private and neutral ground. Of course he wouldn't have known Priya would decide to show up that night. In fact was already there upstairs when Benson and Callahan arrived.

Callahan and Benson had been arguing in the main room of Macmillan Hall, Callahan confessed to police, when Benson heard a noise – that would be Priya – and saw a light come on. Callahan got scared and hurried out the door.

He was clear to the police on that. He made sure they knew he had nothing to do with Priya's death. In fact, Callahan hadn't even stuck around long enough to find out who was upstairs. He just got the hell out. It wasn't until seeing the obituary online on Saturday that he'd put two and two together and figured Benson had probably caused her death.

It was Benson I'd seen Callahan arguing with on the deck of the yacht club. Callahan was scared that Benson would try to put the blame on him for killing Priya. And he wanted none of that.

Benson had not budged after fighting with Callahan at the yacht club. Callahan had threatened to expose him and demanded more money. But Benson had told him he was done paying Callahan's extortion. He'd get no more money. None. Benson had effectively called Callahan's bluff, confident he could brazen out any allegations the young thief could throw at him.

Which is why Callahan had broken into the yacht club. Smashing glass and stealing trophies in hopes they would be valuable. Or if not, at least inflicting some damage at Benson's pretentious hangout.

Callahan also confessed that he'd gone back to the church late Wednesday, scratched up the lock and broken that basement window. So it *was* just my imagination when I thought I'd seen him hurrying away from the church on Thursday morning. Not his brightest move, but he was trying for distraction, to make it look like some random burglar had been the one there the night that Priya died. Benson hadn't put him up to that particular job. Callahan had dreamt it up himself. Not the sharpest knife in the drawer. But by then Callahan was desperate.

Desperation probably also explained his clumsy attempt to run me over in my kayak on Friday morning. Whether he was really trying to drown me or just put a scare into me or was just lashing out in anger, I'm not sure. I guess after his argument with Benson and seeing me out on the water, he wasn't sure how much I'd overheard and how much I knew about what he'd done. He was afraid I knew too much and might figure out what had happened. He wasn't entirely wrong about that.

"OK, Sandra," I said when she'd finished telling me all this. "What do we do now?

"We take this to the city editor and then with her to the

editor-in-chief. We need to bring them into the loop. If even half of this is true, it's a huge story. But like last time, it's also a huge gamble. We'll want to make sure the paper will back us on this."

So we grabbed the city editor and brought her up to speed. Then knocked on the EIC's door.

"Hey, Greg," Sandra said, "we need to talk with you. You're going to want to hear this."

Chapter 27

Let the proud be confounded, for they go wickedly
about to destroy me. But I will be occupied in thy precepts.

– Ps. 119, v. 78

This was going to be Sandra's story. A big one. A scandal almost as big as Gascoyne. Or really just an extension of the Gascoyne scandal, with new players and more background.

And more victims.

I had no desire to write that story. Sandra is a good reporter, and she'd laid it out clearly and persuasively to the *Gazette* editors. It would need to be lawyered, but they agreed to go ahead with it.

It was going to be another long Friday night. I hoped Maggie's had the coffee on.

I knew the story was in capable hands. Sandra deserves it. And anyway I was too close to it. I may no longer be a journalist, at least not officially, but now the Gascoyne mess had slopped over onto my other job as a lowly church musician. The scandal may have begun at big St. Nicholas, but now Benson had dragged that mud over to little St. Quentin.

But just because I wasn't going to write the story didn't mean I couldn't try to help out on background. I'd have to be careful not to cross any legal or ethical lines, not do anything to compromise the *Gazette*'s ability to get the story and expose the guilty parties. But there was nothing stopping me from asking a few questions. After all, I had a personal stake in this too.

I thought of all Gascoyne's victims, both the quick and the dead. I thought of Tommy Holby and others like him – the ones I knew and even the ones I didn't – whose lives were ruined, who were still trying to deal with the trauma Gascoyne and his enablers had inflicted on them and remained responsible for. I thought of my friend Tommy's sister and all the others who weren't themselves directly victims of Gascoyne and his protectors, but who nevertheless in many ways had also suffered hurt and sorrow and pain because of everything those bastards had done.

And of course I thought of Priya, whose death also linked back to Gascoyne's crimes and their coverup.

I couldn't magically take their pain away, couldn't magically bring Priya back to life. But maybe I could help bring them all some closure, some justice. Afflict the comfortable in order to comfort the afflicted. If I confronted Benson directly, maybe I'd learn more. Maybe even persuade him to turn himself in and confess. Worth a shot.

Gotta love small towns. I knew Benson's law office was on the second floor of a building on the west side of the market square that faced toward the back of city hall and kitty corner to the *Gazette*. Walking out the front door of the newspaper after our meeting, I could look over and see his office. And since by now it was well past dinner time and already dark, I could see a light on in the window.

Maybe he was there, working late. Might as well check.

The door to the building on the ground floor was not locked. Overconfident, or just careless? Walking up the steps to the second floor, I found a door with a window of frosted glass and "Benson Law LLC" in gold lettering. That door was also unlocked and led me to an outer office with a desk, phone and computer. Also a plush couch, a coffee table and a few chairs. For clients to wait in, I guess.

But no secretary. Probably sent home for the day. Maybe not part of the job description to lock the downstairs front door. Nor the office, for that matter.

No light in the outer office, but I could see light through the bottom of a door that likely led to Benson's private office. Solid door. No glass there, frosted or otherwise.

I could be polite, knock and announce myself. But knowing what I knew about Benson, I saw no need for the niceties of civil society. So I just walked in and closed the door behind me.

Benson was in a plush leather-and-wood swivel chair reading some papers on his desk, a grand old mahogany piece with carved legs. A brass desk lamp with a Tiffany shade offered the only light. Classy. Opulent. Pretentious.

Benson looked up. If he was startled or worried to see me, he hid it well. He didn't bother to get up from his seat, keeping the big, heavy desk between us.

"Dugan. This is a surprise. What brings you here? What can I do for you? Problem at the church?"

You could say that, I thought. A big problem.

But what I said instead was this:

"I'm here about your friend Patrick Callahan."

"Sorry, who? I don't think I know that name."

"Sure you do, Benson. Tall guy, lanky. Young. Full head of red hair. Drives a mean speedboat."

"Seriously, Dugan. I don't know who you're talking about."

"Really?" I said. "OK, counsellor. Or councillor. Let me refresh your memory."

I took my cellphone out of my pocket and found the audio file, the copy I'd made off Priya's MP3 player, which Sandra and the *Gazette* editors had safely in hand back in the newsroom. I pushed Play. Even with its tiny speaker, Benson's office filled with music, the opening bars of *And He Shall Purify*, from Handel's *Messiah*.

"Ah, *Messiah*. Very nice," he said over the music, all innocent. "The choir is singing that for Christmas, aren't they?"

"Keep listening."

A few more bars went by, and then an abrupt change. The sound of two angry voices arguing. Voices I knew now to be Benson and Callahan:

Benson: – you little prick, you try to blackmail me? I could crush you!

Callahan: Go ahead and try, asshole! What have you got on me? A few minor break-ins – all on your orders anyway.

Benson: Don't forget arson. And probably negligent homicide. A hobo died in that fire.

Callahan: Sure, I burned down that old cottage, but you told me to do it. I didn't know there'd be anybody inside. If I'm guilty of killing him, so are you.

Benson: Not that I'm admitting to anything, but fine. Why don't we just call it even and move on with our lives? You've got to admit our little arrangement has been profitable for you.

Callahan: You're forgetting one thing. I know all about you and that bastard choirmaster at St. Nick's. That prick

174 · DAVID W. BARBER

was abusing choirboys and you knew about. You helped cover it up. For years!

Benson: I knew nothing about that.

Callahan: Bullshit! That fucker diddled my little brother. And my brother told you about it. Mr. big and important churchgoer. Neil was just a kid. He thought you were an authority figure and he could trust you to do something to stop it. To protect him and the other choirboys.

Benson: I'm afraid you're mistaken, Callahan. Your brother told me no such thing.

Callahan: Bullshit again! He left me a note when he died. Told me all about it. His drug overdose wasn't accidental. He killed himself. He just couldn't take the pain anymore. So he found a way out. He was 11 years old, for Christ's sake! I've been sitting on this for years. But not anymore. So you're gonna pay me whatever money I want whenever I want it. Or I take all this to the cops.

Benson: You wouldn't dare, you little shitbag! Wait. Shut up! What's that? –

I stopped the recording. The argument ended there anyway and the music broke back in. I figure Priya had been upstairs listening to *Messiah* on her MP3 player with earbuds, just going over the music in her head. And sitting in the dark, which she liked to do.

When the argument got loud enough for her to hear and she realized what it meant, God love her she'd switched the MP3 player to record. But she must have decided it was too risky for her to stick around. She wanted to leave, but that probably meant turning on the light. And she must have made a noise that startled Benson, so she turned the recorder off and put that in her purse, hoping to sneak away somehow. Part of me wished she'd kept it recording.

On the other hand, I had no desire to hear what must have happened next.

Chapter 28

His speech was smoother than butter, yet war was in his heart.
His words were softer than oil, yet be they very swords.
— Ps. 55, v. 21

"So what happened, Benson? You found Priya upstairs and you realized she'd overheard all your dirty little secrets? What did you do? Threaten her? Try to bribe her? She wouldn't have stood for either of those. She had way too much character and integrity. Not like you."

"I tried to reason with her, of course," Benson said smoothly.

"But she wouldn't listen," he said, his voice still soft. "We were standing at the top of the stairs. And, yes, our discussion got a little heated. She turned to leave and she must have tripped, lost her footing. And she fell down the stairs. I had nothing to do with it."

"Bullshit!" I said. "That seems to be the word of the day."

"It's true!" Benson said.

Pleading now, a bit of whining in his voice. Not a man who was used to being contradicted.

"So let me guess the rest," I said. "Callahan took off, got the hell out of there. He wanted nothing to do with another death. You were still in the upstairs room, so you grabbed Priya's coat and purse and put them beside her body at the bottom of the stairs, so it would look like she was leaving the hall. Hoping we'd all assume she just tripped and fell.

"Did you even check first to see if she might be still alive?

No, you probably didn't. You just left her there. Like the uncaring bastard you are."

Benson didn't say anything. His face was a stone mask. I couldn't tell what he was thinking for feeling. Maybe he never feels anything.

"But you made a mistake, Benson," I said. "Three, actually. First, somehow in the struggle with Priya, you lost a brass button off your fancy navy-blue commodore's jacket. You may have noticed later and had it replaced by now with a new one. But I have the one from the church that I'm pretty sure must be yours. And maybe there will be some of Priya's DNA on it. The police can check that.

"Second, when you left the building, you turned off the light in the vestibule at the bottom of the stairs, probably just out of habit. Or so as not to draw attention to the building.

"And third – probably also out of habit, or maybe to prevent anyone finding the body before you could get safely away – you locked the door to Macmillan Hall after you. You should have had your buddy Carrot Top smash the lock to make it look like a burglary. He scratched the lock and broke a window later on his own, just to try to confuse us."

"You can't prove any of this," Benson said, more confident now, sliding into courtroom lawyer mode. "This is all just supposition. Circumstantial."

"I've got the recording," I said.

"Inadmissible," Benson said dismissively. "I could get any judge to throw that out. Easily."

"It won't be as easy as that, Benson. We have the recording, we have Callahan's testimony, we likely have his brother's suicide note. That should be more than enough to at least convince the police to launch a proper investigation.

"Besides, now that we know for certain there was a big coverup of Gascoyne's crimes, I'm sure the fine reporters and editors at the *Gazette* will be able to dig up even more evidence of your guilt and that of any others.

"The truth will come out, Benson. It usually does, with some help."

Benson leaned forward in his big swivel chair and put his palms flat on the expensive mahogany desk.

"But I was protecting the church! He raised his voice. "Protecting its reputation!"

"More important than protecting children?"

"But we were doing good work!"

"Sure," I said. "A lot of it's good. But what about all the bad stuff?"

Benson stood up, his hands still on the desk.

"But, but – we had a soup kitchen. A homeless shelter. We helped immigrant families!"

His face was getting red, a drop of spittle at the edge of his mouth.

Rage. Frustration. Whatever.

"You're right," I said. "The church does do some good work. Maybe a lot. And every Christmas, the biker gangs deliver teddy bears to little kids. Doesn't mean the rest of the year those biker gangs aren't mostly doing drugs, extortion and sex trafficking."

"But our reputation!"

He was back on that one.

Benson took a breath, adjusted his tie and gave a tiny twist of his head. Calmed his voice.

The learned lawyer making his case to an imaginary courtroom.

"I was protecting the church and the choir," Benson said. "That choir was famous. You know that.

"It brought us a lot of prestige. Not just to the church, but to the whole town. People came from all over to Grayston to hear the choir. And they stayed in our hotels and spent money in our stores and restaurants."

"Sure," I said. "And probably put a lot of money into the church coffers too. But so what? At what cost?"

"The Reverend Canon Chandler and I were protecting the church. We knew what was best for her. The choir was her biggest asset. With Julian Gascoyne gone, it's nothing now. And now you come around trying to dig up old dirt and damage our reputation all over again.

"I couldn't have that," he said. "Couldn't risk you sticking your meddling journalist nose into things."

"You don't know jack, Jack!"

Now I was shouting too. I got quieter.

"You and Chandler and anyone else who helped cover up the sexual abuse of children, you're not Christians," I said.

"It's an insult to the faith for you to call yourselves that. And you're certainly not caring members of your community."

Benson started to speak, but I plowed on over him.

"What Gascoyne did to those children was sick and perverted, no question. Some of them died, by suicide or got lost into drugs and overdoses."

I thought of young Neil Callahan, Carrot Top's little brother, a Gascoyne victim. Of Tommy Holby, my friend's brother.

And I thought of all the other victims, both the dead and those still living in pain.

"That's tragic," I said. "But the worse fate may be the ones who survived. Battered, abused, broken.

"Some of Gascoyne's victims – no, let me correct that: victims of Gascoyne and you and Chandler and all of you self-important, self-righteous bastards who covered for him – some of those survivors and their families have courageously rebuilt their lives and tried to move on.

"But others haven't been so successful at doing that. You can see them all around Grayston and beyond if you know what signs to look for.

"Even for the strongest survivors," I said, "the damage you all inflicted will haunt them forever. Maybe death would be kinder, rather than a living hell for the rest of their lives."

Bare ruin'd choirs, where late the sweet birds sang.

Benson sat back down. Waved his hand to dismiss me. Clearly, I was a mere annoyance and unworthy of his time.

"Here's the thing, Benson," I said. "Here's what you don't get: Gascoyne is a pedophile. I don't pretend to understand that – and I'm certainly not condoning his actions. But somehow in some way he's sick in the head. His brain chemistry's off. The wiring's messed up. Something's gone wrong. I'm not excusing him, but at some level he probably can't help himself. Can't control his urges.

"But you – you and Chandler and anyone else who had a hand in this big, shameful coverup – you don't have that excuse."

I was getting louder again.

"You're just ethically corrupt. And morally bankrupt. All

you care about is your money and prestige and your precious reputation.

"Well, that's all gone now, Benson. You can kiss that goodbye. All of you. The *Gazette* already has the story. And this little conversation we've had will just add more detail. It's as good as a confession. I'll testify to that. Gladly. Your money, your power, your status in this town – all gone.

"You're going to prison, Jack. For a long time. For enabling a pedophile. For murder. And for all your other crimes.

"You and Gascoyne can share a cell. And you can both rot in hell."

I didn't hear Benson open the desk drawer.

But I sure as hell saw the gun in his hand. Pointing right at me.

I hate guns. They scare me at the best of times. Which clearly this wasn't.

"I don't think so, Dugan," Benson said.

It bothered me that he'd used my first name. I didn't want to be friendly with this bastard.

"Most of the so-called 'evidence' you have against me is circumstantial at best," Benson said. "Or based on the testimony of a two-bit thief. Who's going to believe him over me? Nobody. I'm a respected lawyer."

"Circumstantial?" I showed him the cellphone in my hand. "I have a recording of you arguing with Patrick Callahan. That supports his testimony pretty strongly."

"A minor problem at best," Benson said. "You just hand that over to me and I can make it go away. As you say, I have some experience in covering up uncomfortable truths."

Damn! I wish I'd thought to set it to record. He'd just confessed again. Too late now. But I wasn't about to surrender it to him, even with that nasty gun still pointing at me.

"I don't think so, Benson," I said, stowing the phone safely in my pocket.

"Don't worry," I said, "I'm sure everything will come out at the trial. There will be plenty of evidence to convict you."

"Don't forget I've got the gun," Benson said, giving it a little waggle.

"Sure, you've got the gun," I said, hoping I sounded more brave than I felt. "But I don't think you've got the guts.

"You can have your lackey kill a homeless man in a fire, or you can push a woman down some stairs to her death –"

"– I told you that was an accident!"

"No, I think it was murder. I think you pushed her at the top of the stairs and you didn't care what happened next. And she fell down those stairs and she hit her head and broke her neck.

"If Priya's death really *was* an accident," I said, "you should have called the police and stuck around. But you have too much to hide, don't you? And ethics are clearly not your strong suit.

"So you might be willing to have a hand in someone's death, you sack of shit. But to shoot someone standing right in front of you? I don't think so."

I turned to leave. Hoping to hell I was right, that Benson was too much of a coward to shoot me. Especially in the back. He was happy to have someone else do his dirty work, but not one to get his own hands dirty.

I was walking, not running. The five or so steps from

Benson's fancy desk to the door out of his office didn't take me long to cover. They just felt like forever. But I got through the door and closed it behind me. I stood there for a moment, waiting. Not sure what for. Maybe just another hunch.

It didn't take long. I heard the sound of the gun firing and the thump of something hitting the desk.

I think I knew what.

I opened the door back into Benson's office, pretty sure of what I would find.

I was not wrong.

John ("call me Jack") Benson – prominent Grayston lawyer, church warden, blackmailer, pedophile enabler, accessory to at least two murders and several other tragic deaths in this quiet little town – was slumped at his desk. What was left of his head lay in a spreading pool of blood that was marring the nice mahogany surface.

So much blood.

The gun was probably somewhere on the carpet below him.

I'd let the cops find it. That's their job.

I called my friend Don Patterson and told him to come over with his team. I told him there was no rush. I'd be waiting here for them to arrive. Then I called Sandra at the *Gazette* to give her the scoop.

There was no point calling for an ambulance.

Benson had put the gun in his mouth and pulled the trigger. The lower half of his face was missing, his smug smile gone forever.

The messiest kind of hedshot.

About the Author

David W. Barber is a journalist and musician and the author of more than a dozen books of music (including *Accidentals on Purpose*; *Bach, Beethoven and the Boys*; *When the Fat Lady Sings;* and *Getting a Handel on Messiah*) and literature (including *Quotable Sherlock*, *Quotable Alice* and *Atonement and other stories*). Formerly a writer and entertainment editor of *The Kingston Whig-Standard*, editor of *Broadcast Week* magazine at the Toronto *Globe and Mail* and the assistant editor of arts and life for Postmedia newspapers, he is currently a freelance writer, editor, musician and composer. As a composer, his works include two symphonies, a jazz mass based on the music of Dave Brubeck, a *Requiem*, several short choral and chamber works and various vocal-jazz songs and arrangements. He sings with the Toronto Chamber Choir and various other choirs on occasion. In a varied career, among his more interesting jobs have been short stints as a roadie for Pope John Paul II, a publicist for Prince Rainier of Monaco and a backup singer for Avril Lavigne.

Learn about his other books at IndentPublishing.com

Books by David W. Barber
with illustrations by Dave Donald

Available in print and/or as ebooks
from Indent Publishing

A Musician's Dictionary
(1983)
(Revised and expanded in 2011 as
Accidentals on Purpose: A Musician's Dictionary)

Bach, Beethoven and the Boys:
Music History as It Ought to Be Taught
(1986, revised 2021)

When the Fat Lady Sings:
Opera History as It Ought to Be Taught
(1990)

If It Ain't Baroque:
More Music History as It Ought to Be Taught
(1992)

Getting a Handel on Messiah
(1995)

Tutus, Tights and Tiptoes:
Ballet History as It Ought to Be Taught
(2000)

Other Books by
David W. Barber

The Last Laugh:
Essays and Oddities in the News
(2000)

Quotable Alice
(2001)

Quotable Sherlock
(2001)

Quotable Twain
(2002)

The Adventure of the Sunken Parsley:
and Other Stories of Sherlock Holmes
(2011)

Better Than it Sounds:
The Music Lover's Quotation Book
(2013)

Think Again!
by Leo Tolstoy, with annotations and commentary
by David W. Barber
(2022)

Atonement and other stories
(2022)

Leacock Laughter
(2023)

Other Books by
Indent Publishing

Learn to Play
(2022)

A Feast of Wolves
(2023)

Wilds Strawberries Along the Mackenzie
(2023)

Find all Indent books at our website:
IndentPublishing.com